A Tail of Terror!

Maggie loves her new dog, Poocher. He's cute, sweet, and likes to cuddle up in Maggie's lap to take a nap.

Maggie thinks Poocher is the greatest dog in the world.

Until he starts changing. His cute little bark becomes a deep, booming "woof!" His fangs get longer. His claws grow sharper. And his fur turns *green!*

Suddenly Maggie's afraid that her new doggy has a bite much worse than his bark!

Also from R.L. Stine

The Beast®
The Beast® 2

R.L. Stine's Ghosts of Fear Street
#1 Hide and Shriek
#2 Who's Been Sleeping in My Grave?
#3 Attack of the Aqua Apes
#4 Nightmare in 3-D
#5 Stay Away from the Tree House
#6 Eye of the Fortuneteller
#7 Fright Knight
#8 The Ooze
#9 Revenge of the Shadow People
#10 The Bugman Lives!
#11 The Boy Who Ate Fear Street
#12 Night of the Werecat
#13 How to Be a Vampire
#14 Body Switchers from Outer Space
#15 Fright Christmas
#16 Don't Ever Get Sick at Granny's
#17 House of a Thousand Screams
#18 Camp Fear Ghouls
#19 Three Evil Wishes
#20 Spell of the Screaming Jokers
#21 The Creature from Club Lagoona
#22 Field of Screams
#23 Why I'm Not Afraid of Ghosts

Available from MINSTREL Books

For orders other than by individual consumers, Pocket Books grants a discount on the purchase of **10 or more** copies of single titles for special markets or premium use. For further details, please write to the Vice-President of Special Markets, Pocket Books, 1633 Broadway, New York, NY 10019-6785, 8th Floor.

For information on how individual consumers can place orders, please write to Mail Order Department, Simon & Schuster Inc., 200 Old Tappan Road, Old Tappan, NJ 07675.

R·L·STINE'S GHOSTS OF FEAR STREET®

MONSTER DOG

A Parachute Press Book

A MINSTREL® BOOK

PUBLISHED BY POCKET BOOKS

New York London Toronto Sydney Tokyo Singapore

A MINSTREL PAPERBACK *Original*

A Minstrel Paperback published by
POCKET BOOKS, a division of Simon & Schuster Inc.
1230 Avenue of the Americas, New York, NY 10020

MONSTER DOG WRITTEN BY RICK SURMACZ

ISBN: 0-671-00853-6

First Minstrel Books paperback printing September 1997

10 9 8 7 6 5 4 3 2 1

Cover art by Broeck Steadman

Printed in the U.S.A.

R·L·STINE'S
GHOSTS OF FEAR STREET®

MONSTER DOG

1

The beast waits for me every day after school.

It hides in the bushes along Fear Street. It licks its teeth. It sharpens its claws.

It waits just for me.

I never know exactly where it will hide. I never know when it will attack.

But I know it's there.

And it wants to get me.

"Once again, Maggie Clark was the only student who managed to get a perfect grade on the last homework assignment," Mr. Gosling announced to the class. He beamed at me.

I sank farther into my seat. I felt my face grow

warm. Don't blush! I ordered myself furiously. That will only make it worse.

"Little Miss Perfect does it again," Billy Caldwell whispered behind me. Someone giggled.

Luckily the bell rang. Phew! Just in time. I could tell from the way Mr. Gosling smiled that he was about to say something even more embarrassing about me.

I know he means well—but all his compliments are *killing* me!

Mr. Gosling reminded the class to read chapter ten in our science books. All the kids jumped up from their seats and rushed to their lockers. Everyone was thrilled that school was over for the week.

Except me.

Because now it was time to walk home.

And I knew—the beast was waiting.

I trudged through the crowded hallway. Pushing my way to my locker, I organized my schoolbooks.

Someone shouted my name. "Maggie!"

I turned and gazed past a sea of students. My best friend Judy was ambling toward me. She's hard to miss. She's the tallest kid in the whole sixth grade, and she has bright red hair. Just the opposite of me. I'm kind of short, with long, curly dark hair.

"Happy birthday!" Judy greeted me. "Ready to go home and open your presents?"

I nodded weakly. Turning twelve was fun.

Getting home was the scary part.

But I hid my fear from Judy. I already had sort of a wimpy reputation. It went with being teacher's pet.

Not that I *try* to be teacher's pet. It just happens.

"I wish I didn't have so much homework on my birthday," I complained.

Judy eyed the pile of books in my arms. "Knowing you, you'll knock it all off before dinner. And then volunteer to do extra chores or something."

"Oh, stop." I rolled my eyes. "I'm not that bad." I slammed my locker and turned around. "I mean *good.*"

I followed Judy out through the front doors of Shadyside Middle School. The sidewalk was filled with students. We wove through the crowd and headed toward Hawthorne Drive.

"So do you know what you're getting? Anything special?" Judy asked.

I smiled. As a matter of fact, I *did* know. "Yeah—I think it's something pretty special," I replied.

Judy grabbed my arm. "What? A CD player? A TV for your room? Tell me!"

"Come over for some birthday cake after dinner," I offered. "I'll show you."

Judy sighed. "Oh, all right. But I hate it when you do this to me, Maggie," she complained.

Judy always wants to know everything right away. I tease her by keeping secrets.

We kept walking. Down Hawthorne. Right on Park.

My stomach tightened as we approached my street.

Fear Street.

Where the beast lived.

We reached Judy's house, right near the corner of Fear Street and Park Drive. "Well, here I am, birthday girl." Judy shifted her book bag to her other shoulder. "See you around seven o'clock."

I turned toward Fear Street. I took a step forward, then hesitated.

I guess Judy noticed. "What's wrong?" she asked.

I hugged my schoolbooks. "Nothing," I mumbled.

I felt my face turn red. For the second time that day.

It was so embarrassing to be afraid. I just turned twelve, after all. I was too old to be such a baby.

"Everything's fine!" I declared. I gave her a big smile and hoped she believed me.

Judy shrugged. "All right. See you later!" She turned and hurried up her front walk.

And I was all alone on Fear Street.

Everything *seemed* calm and peaceful. The sun shone. Birds chirped. Leaves twirled in the trees.

But I knew it was there—waiting for me.

I took a deep breath and hugged my schoolbooks.

"Here I go," I murmured to myself. I took a few steps and stopped.

Something rustled in the bushes.

I froze.

Branches snapped. I took a step backward. My heart went *thump. Thump.*

Something dashed out of the bushes!

I screamed.

Then I saw what it was.

A squirrel. Just a stupid squirrel!

The poor little thing jumped in fright and scampered up a tree. I giggled nervously. Get a grip, Maggie! I told myself.

I studied the entire length of Fear Street.

Nothing but trees and grass and sunshine.

I sucked in a deep breath and marched down the street. I glared at every bush I passed. I expected the beast to jump out at me any second.

But it didn't.

"Okay," I whispered. "Almost home."

I didn't have to be afraid of that crummy beast. Not anymore.

Then something growled behind me.

I clutched my schoolbooks so tightly my knuckles hurt. Slowly I turned around. My heart raced.

Something moved in the shrubbery near the sidewalk. Something big.

I stepped backward. "N-nice boy," I stammered. "G-good boy."

The thing in the shrubs moved.

Then it attacked!

I screamed as the beast lunged out of the shrubbery.

Bullhead!

The biggest, ugliest, meanest dog on Fear Street!

And he was coming after me!

I shrieked and ran.

The massive bulldog snarled and snapped at my ankles. His huge, hideous head bobbed up and down. His sloppy, wet tongue flopped from side to side.

"No, Bullhead, no!" I screamed.

My sneakers slapped against the sidewalk. My hair flew in my face. I could hardly see where I was going, but I didn't care. I had to get away from Bullhead.

The big bulldog's sharp toenails clicked on the sidewalk behind me. He was getting closer.

I flew forward, even faster. "I'm almost home," I chanted under my breath. "Almost home . . . almost home . . ."

I spotted my house in the distance. The front porch. The oak tree. The white picket fence.

Home!

I glanced over my shoulder as I bolted across the street.

Bullhead was right behind me!

I was going to have to dive over the fence. It was my only chance.

I dashed forward and threw my books over the fence. Then I leaped into the air.

Up, up, and over . . .

Until something tugged at my leg.

Bullhead.

His jaws clamped around my ankle!

2

Bullhead sank his teeth into my jeans. The fabric tore away from my ankle. I fell forward and tumbled onto the lawn.

Safe!

Bullhead threw himself against the fence and barked angrily.

I stood up and stared down at him.

The beast glared back at me with his mean little bulldog eyes. He chomped greedily on the ripped piece of my jeans.

"Go ahead and chew on that, you nasty mutt!" I yelled at Bullhead. "You're not going to get a piece of me!"

Bullhead growled.

"Just you wait, Bullhead," I warned, seething.

"Today is my birthday, and I'm getting a dog even bigger and meaner than you!"

Someone snickered.

"Yeah, right," a voice jeered.

Billy Caldwell stepped out from behind a tree.

I call him Billy the Bully. Not only do I have to put up with him at school—he has to live next door to me too!

Billy is Bullhead's mean, ugly owner. I don't know who is meaner or uglier, Billy or Bullhead. They could almost be twins, except one is a dog and the other is a boy. Both are stocky with weird, squashed-in faces, short legs, and even shorter tempers.

"Admit it, Billy," I accused him. "You trained Bullhead to hate me!"

Billy scoffed. "I don't know what you're talking about."

"You'd better watch it," I threatened. I glared over the fence. "I'm getting my own dog to protect me."

"No wimpy dog of yours could ever scare us," Billy boasted. "Right, Bullhead?"

Bullhead wagged his tail and barked.

"We'll see," I huffed as I picked up my schoolbooks. "Just wait until you both meet Killer."

Bullhead dropped the shredded piece of my jeans and stared at me.

"Killer?" Billy echoed. His wide grin faded a little.

"Killer," I repeated. "Mom took me to the dog pound last week, and I picked out the biggest, meanest dog for my birthday present. And guess what? Today is my birthday!"

Now Billy looked worried. Good.

"No way," he blustered. "No dog is tougher than Bullhead!"

I leaned over the fence and whispered into Billy's ear, "Killer eats bulldogs for breakfast."

Then I turned and marched toward the house. I felt much better. Let Billy be scared for a change.

When I stepped through the front door, Mom and Dad greeted me with a bouquet of colored balloons. My little brother Peter tossed confetti at me.

"Happy birthday, Maggie!" they all shouted.

I scanned the room quickly for a glimpse of my present—the greatest present in the world.

Where was Killer?

He wasn't in the living room. All I saw was the television and the green sofa and the round coffee table with Mom's favorite vase in the center.

Mom must have noticed me glancing around. "Presents *after* dinner," she told me.

"After dinner? Don't know if I can wait that long!"

"You'll manage. I made all your favorites," Mom added. "Spaghetti with meat sauce, garlic bread, and broccoli."

I sighed. "Sounds great," I murmured. "Well, I guess I might as well start on my homework now."

I turned and headed up the stairs to my room.

"Maggie!" Mom gasped. "What happened to your jeans? The leg is ripped!"

I couldn't tell her about Bullhead. I was too embarrassed. No one else seemed to have a problem with that stupid dog.

Mom says Bullhead picks on me because he knows I'm afraid. She told me dogs can smell fear.

If that's true—I must really stink!

"It's nothing," I mumbled. "An accident. It'll never happen again."

Not with Killer around to protect me!

It was hard, but I managed to survive until after dinner. We ate at the picnic table in the yard. When Judy arrived, Mom brought out the cake. I blew out the candles and made a wish.

I wished for the biggest, meanest, scariest guard dog on Fear Street.

"Can I open my presents now?" I burst out. I gazed longingly at a large, pointed object draped in a big yellow sheet in the corner of the yard. It was topped with a red bow.

It had to be Killer's doghouse!

Mom handed around slices of cake. "Open these first," she ordered, placing a stack of wrapped boxes on the table.

I tore through those presents so quickly, I almost ripped in half the book Mom and Dad gave me. The only present I really wanted was waiting for me under that yellow sheet.

My Killer!

Only one small wrapped package left. I opened it quickly. It was a new video game. Alien Death Squad.

"Gee, thanks," I mumbled. Usually, I liked playing video games a lot. But right then I couldn't care less about it.

Peter's eyes lit up. "Alien Death Squad?" he

whooped. "Cool! That's my favorite game. Come on, Maggie! Let's play a round!"

I gave him an annoyed glance. "Not right now."

Peter is eight years old. He can be a real pain sometimes.

"You can play later, Peter," Mom told him. "Maggie has one more present to open."

Peter frowned and slumped back in his chair.

I jumped up and ran across the lawn. I reached down and lifted the yellow sheet.

Yes! A doghouse!

I pulled the sheet away and marveled at the beautiful new doghouse. It was painted white with blue trim to match our house.

And I heard something panting inside.

Killer!

I crouched down on my hands and knees.

"Here, Killer," I crooned. "Come on out, boy!"

Nothing.

I crawled to the door of the little house.

"Come on, doggy," I whispered. "That's a good boy."

Something whimpered in the dark.

"Killer?" I murmured. "Are you okay?"

I peered into the doghouse.

And screamed.

3

I couldn't believe my eyes.

Inside the doghouse was the tiniest little puppy I had ever seen!

It wasn't a "Killer" at all. It was an itty-bitty brown fur ball, small enough to cradle in my hands.

I turned to face my parents, in shock.

"Maggie, what's wrong?" Dad asked.

I reached into the doghouse and pulled out the little brown puppy. The tiny dog squirmed in my hands.

"Does this look like a 'Killer' to you?" I demanded. "You got the wrong dog! You were supposed to pick up Killer at the pound!"

Mom shrugged. "I'm sorry, Maggie," she explained. "Killer's owner showed up to claim him. And it's just as well, honey. He was much too big to take care of. He would eat us out of house and home."

I held up the little dog. My friend Judy squealed with delight. "He's so cute, Maggie!" she cried.

"Yeah, cute," I muttered.

It was the most pathetic little puppy I'd ever seen! Bullhead would swallow him up in one gulp!

How embarrassing!

"All right, he's not Killer, but he's still a dog," Dad commented. "You said you wanted a dog."

I sighed. How could they think this pipsqueak puppy was as good as Killer?

The little brown puppy squirmed in my arms. He was so tiny! How could I protect myself against Bullhead with this . . . this . . . ball of fluff?

"His name is Poocher," Mom informed us. "That's what they called him at the dog pound."

Peter snickered.

"Poocher?" I echoed. Oh, man! What would Billy Caldwell say when he heard *that?*

"Maggie, he'll grow. You'll see," Mom went on. "Puppies grow very quickly. Who knows how big Poocher will get? He's a mixed breed, after all. He might surprise you."

I slumped down on the lawn with Poocher in my arms. "He surprised me, all right," I mumbled.

The little dog jumped off my lap and rolled in the grass.

Judy burst out laughing. She must have startled him, because the little puppy froze on the spot. He stared at us with his huge brown eyes. His ears flopped across his head.

Judy laughed. "He's adorable, Maggie!" she gushed.

I had to admit, she was right.

"Poocher," I whispered.

The puppy jumped up on his back legs and yipped. He recognized his name.

I glanced up at Mom and Dad. "That's his bark?"

They nodded.

Well, it wouldn't scare Bullhead or Billy.

But it might make them laugh themselves to death!

"Yip! Yip! Yip!" Poocher danced on his back legs and twirled around faster and faster. He tumbled onto the grass. I rubbed his furry belly, and he yipped with delight.

"What a great little dog!" Judy exclaimed.

"He's okay, I guess," I admitted.

"Let's see if he'll eat some birthday cake," Judy suggested.

"Come on, Poocher," I called.

The little puppy jumped into my arms and licked my face. It tickled and made me giggle.

I wanted to hate him. He wasn't Killer, after all.

But really—how could I hate a little puppy?

I carried Poocher to the picnic table and sat down next to Judy. Scooping up a little piece of cake, I held it to Poocher's mouth.

He sniffed it curiously. Then he wolfed it down in one quick bite.

He liked it!

Poocher yipped happily as I sliced off a corner with

lots of frosting. When he finished the cake, he curled up into a ball on my lap and closed his eyes. In seconds, he was asleep.

"He's so sweet," Judy whispered.

Poocher's little furry belly rose and fell as he snored. My heart melted. I couldn't help myself. I was falling in love with the little thing.

Who cared what Billy and his stupid Bullhead thought? Poocher was mine. My very own puppy.

Peter tapped me on the shoulder.

"What do you want?" I asked softly. I didn't want to wake Poocher.

"You didn't open *my* present," Peter complained. He handed me a square box wrapped in aluminum foil. "Open it!"

I slowly slid my hand away from Poocher. The puppy yawned and shifted, but he didn't wake up.

Carefully I tore the foil off the square box. I lifted the cardboard lid.

My breath stopped.

A tangle of snakes lay coiled inside the box. Staring up at me. Their fangs gleamed.

Before I could even move, they struck at my face!

4

The snakes flew straight at me!

I screamed and threw the box in the air. Snakes rained down around me. Their scaly bodies wriggled. Ugh!

Poocher jumped up, barking wildly. I clutched him in my arms and climbed onto my chair.

"Ha-ha!" Peter burst out laughing. He clasped his hands over his stomach and bent over. "Ha-ha-ha! They're only rubber snakes. I can't believe you fell for it. You thought they were real!"

Rubber? I stared at the snakes on the lawn.

They weren't moving.

"Peter!" I yelled. I climbed off the chair and sat down again. My face turned bright red.

Judy and my parents started laughing.

Laughing at me! I couldn't believe it!

Poocher cowered on my lap. His little body trembled.

"Look what you did, Peter!" I snapped. "You scared Poocher!"

"Ex-cuuuuse me." Peter rolled his eyes.

I hugged Poocher and tried to calm him down. "I wish *you* were my little brother," I told him. "You'd never play such a stupid trick. Would you, puppy?"

Still smiling, Mom cut herself a slice of cake. "Maybe we should send Peter to Dr. Diller's Dog Clinic too," she joked.

My jaw dropped. "Dog clinic? What dog clinic?"

"It's nothing to worry about," Mom explained. "On Monday we have to take Poocher to Dr. Diller's for his shots and some obedience training. He'll be gone for only a week."

"A week?" I gasped. "A whole week caged up in a dog clinic?"

Poocher seemed to understand. He whimpered and buried his nose under my arm.

"I'm sorry, Maggie," Mom consoled me. "But he has to have his shots. And he could use some training too. One bad boy around here is enough." She winked at Peter.

I hugged Poocher and kissed his furry head. My Poocher trapped in a steel cage for a whole week? What a terrible thought.

"My dog had to get shots too," Judy announced. "When we got to the vet's office, he hid under a chair and wouldn't come out."

"Thanks a lot," I grumbled.

She really knew how to make me feel better!

Judy went home a little while later. It was almost dark out, but I wanted to play with my puppy. "I'm going to teach you to play fetch," I told him.

I ran up to my room and brought down a little rubber ball. The ball looked huge in Poocher's tiny mouth. He could barely carry it. He was so cute!

Mom made me invite Peter to play with us. "I don't want him bothering Poocher," I argued. But Mom insisted.

Of course, practically the first thing Peter did was to toss the ball over the fence. Poocher barked like crazy because he couldn't find it.

"You did that on purpose," I accused Peter.

"Did not," he insisted.

But then he did it again! The ball soared over the fence, and Poocher went nuts.

"If you can't play nice, leave us alone," I snapped.

Peter stomped into the house. What a brat!

On Saturday, Dad installed a doggy door in the back door. Now Poocher could come and go as he pleased.

Poocher was afraid of the little door at first. I held up a dog biscuit to coax him through. I waved the biscuit in front of Poocher's nose. He sniffed and stepped forward. Finally he hopped through the doggy door.

"Good doggy!" I praised him.

Poocher wagged his tail. Then he turned around

and hopped through the door again. And again. And again. Each time, he peered up at me with twinkling brown eyes.

"You sure love to play, don't you?" I said, laughing.

Peter came into the kitchen. "I love to play too," he announced. "Let's play Alien Death Squad."

I sighed. "I'm playing with Poocher now, Peter."

"How about after dinner?" Peter pressed.

"I don't know," I replied. "I have to finish my homework. And Poocher needs a lot of attention."

"Stupid dog," Peter grumbled. He stalked out of the kitchen.

On Sunday, I played tug-of-war with Poocher in the backyard. I used an old towel that Mom gave me. I held on to one end and Poocher sank his teeth into the other end. Then we tugged back and forth.

He was pretty strong for such a little puppy!

Maybe Mom was right. Maybe Poocher would grow up to be big and tough. Tough enough to take on old Bullhead.

Poocher tugged harder on the towel and growled.

"That's it, boy," I encouraged. "Pretend it's Bullhead. Big, mean, nasty dog. That's it! Get him, boy! Get Bullhead!"

Something growled behind the fence.

I'd recognize that awful sound anywhere.

Bullhead.

Poocher dropped the towel and sniffed the air. He stared at the fence fearfully.

I hugged my little puppy. "Don't be afraid, Poocher."

"Poocher?" a voice rang out. "What happened to Killer?"

I glanced up. Billy the Bully sneered at me from behind the fence. He smirked when he saw Poocher in my arms.

"Did you get a pet rat instead of a dog?" he taunted.

"Just wait, Billy," I shot back. "Poocher is going to grow up to be bigger than old Bullhead! He's going to be the best, fiercest dog on Fear Street!"

Billy roared with laughter. "Oh, yeah, right. Bullhead and I are so scared."

Bullhead licked his chops and barked. Then the two of them turned and swaggered off. Billy's laughter echoed in the streets.

I hugged and stroked Poocher. "Don't worry, puppy," I whispered. "I love you anyway—even if you'll never be scary."

Even if you'll never be scary. I didn't know what I was saying then. But I would remember those words later.

I was so wrong!

5

Monday came too fast. All day at school I dreaded taking Poocher to the clinic. But the time finally came.

When Judy and I walked out of school, there was Mom, waiting for us in the parking lot. Poocher jumped up and down on the backseat of our station wagon.

Poocher loved riding in the car. He stuck his furry little head out the window and yipped at the passing traffic.

"Poor puppy!" Judy commented. "He doesn't know he's going to have needles poked into him for the next week."

I glared at her. She came along to cheer me up. So far, it wasn't working.

"Does he have to stay for a whole week?" I whined.

Mom nodded and turned the steering wheel. "I'm afraid so, Maggie. But don't worry. Dr. Diller is one of the finest veterinarians in the country. And Poocher really needs his shots. You don't want him to get sick, do you?"

"No . . . but why a whole week?" I complained.

Mom sighed. "They need to house-train him and teach him some basic commands. Really, Maggie, it's not a big deal at all."

I crossed my arms and stared out the window.

Poocher whimpered softly and licked my face. It tickled.

I giggled and hugged him. "You're a good dog, aren't you, Poocher?" I whispered.

"Yip! Yip! Yip!"

"Look!" Judy pointed out the car window. "There's the dog clinic."

Mom steered the car into a small parking lot. I gazed up at a large gray concrete building.

It looked like a prison.

A gold plaque above the door read DR. DILLER'S DOG CLINIC.

"I don't like this place," I muttered.

Mom parked the car and sighed. "Maggie, please," she scolded. "Stop whining. We have to do this. It's for Poocher's own good."

I gazed into Poocher's brown eyes. "I'm going to miss you, sweetie," I whispered in his ear. Poocher licked my face.

"Come on, Maggie," Mom said gently. "Let's take him inside."

"I'll wait out here," Judy offered. "So you and Poocher can say good-bye in private."

Reluctantly, I attached a leash to Poocher's collar and got out of the car. Poocher pranced up the steps to the front door of the clinic.

Poor Poocher! He didn't know he was going to be caged up for a week.

Mom pushed the buzzer next to the door.

After a few moments, the giant steel door swung open. A tall, friendly-looking woman with gray hair greeted us.

"Hello! I'm Dr. Nina Diller. I've been expecting you," she said. "Please come inside."

Mom and I stepped inside. We gazed down a long hall lined with big steel doors. Poocher sniffed the air curiously. I tugged the leash and led him down the hallway.

It was bright white inside. No color anywhere, except for a bright red door at the end of the hall. Fluorescent lights gleamed on the tile floor. Distant barks echoed through the building.

"You must be Mrs. Clark, and you must be Maggie." Dr. Diller bent down and patted Poocher on the head. "And you must be Poocher!"

"Yip!" Poocher licked her hand.

That made me feel better. Poocher seemed to like her.

Dr. Diller peered at me from behind her glasses and

smiled. She stuck her hands into the pockets of her white lab coat. "Your mom needs to fill out some forms, Maggie," she explained. "You can spend a few more minutes with Poocher, okay?"

I tried to smile, but Dr. Diller noticed my sadness.

"I know how hard it is to give up your puppy for a week," she comforted me. "But don't worry. Poocher will be fine. I'll make him so healthy and happy, you won't even recognize him."

"I like him just the way he is," I mumbled.

Dr. Diller led Mom to a large desk. They sat down and started going over some paperwork.

I slumped into a chair and gazed down sadly at Poocher. He jumped up on my lap and licked my cheek.

"You be a good puppy for Dr. Diller, okay?" I whispered.

Poocher yipped. I hugged him tightly.

"Okay, Maggie," Mom called. "It's time to go."

I placed Poocher on the concrete floor and handed the leash to Dr. Diller. "Bye, Poocher," I said quietly.

Poocher wagged his tail.

Dr. Diller escorted us to the entrance. "Don't worry about Poocher, Maggie," she said as I stepped outside. "I promise I'll take good care of him."

The heavy steel door swung shut with a bang.

Mom and I trudged back to the car. Judy was leaning on the hood, gazing at the clinic.

"What an ugly building," she commented.

I shrugged. "Yeah," I agreed. "But at least Dr. Diller is really nice."

And when Poocher came home, we'd really show that dumb Billy and that dumber Bullhead.

I hoped.

It was the longest week of my life.

I mean, it's not like I sat around moping all week. I was busy with homework and school. Judy and I hung out at the mall on Tuesday night. I even played a couple of rounds of Alien Death Squad with Peter.

But still, I missed Poocher so much!

Now it was Thursday. Two more days to go before Poocher could come home. And I just couldn't stand waiting any longer.

I stood at the kitchen window and stared longingly at the empty doghouse in the yard.

Peter popped his head in the kitchen doorway. "I challenge you to another round of Alien Death Squad!" he announced.

I sighed. "I'm sick of playing Alien Death Squad," I complained. "Anyway, I beat you the last two games."

"I know," Peter admitted. "But this time I challenge you to a super ultimate championship tournament. Whoever wins will rule the universe!"

"You can have the universe." I sighed. "I just want Poocher back."

Disappointment flashed across Peter's face. "Okay, be that way," he grumbled. "That means I rule the universe! Me! I rule!"

He marched around the kitchen chanting "I rule the universe! I rule the universe!"

Little brothers can drive you crazy.

I had to get out of the house. I had to see Poocher.

That was when I got an idea.

A great idea!

6

Why didn't I think of it before?

I could go visit Poocher at the dog clinic!

Dr. Diller wouldn't mind, would she?

Peter marched into the living room, still chanting "I rule the universe." I grabbed my jacket off the hook and opened the back door quietly. I decided not to say anything to Mom and Dad. I'd be back before they missed me anyway.

I stepped outside into the twilight. It was getting dark earlier, and there was a chill in the air. I zipped up my jacket and got my bike out of the garage.

Fear Street was quiet and kind of creepy. It made me nervous. It was *Fear* Street, after all, and it was totally deserted.

I shifted my bike into high gear. My feet pumped

the pedals hard as I flew to the end of Fear Street. I didn't stop until I reached Dr. Diller's Dog Clinic.

I carried my bike up the steps to the front door of the ugly concrete building. After I caught my breath, I pushed the buzzer. Then I waited.

And waited.

And waited.

Nothing.

I buzzed again and gazed up at the barred windows of the clinic.

No lights.

What's going on? I wondered. Is it closed already?

The sun had set, and the sky was dark. The clinic must be closed. Or maybe Dr. Diller was busy and couldn't hear the buzzer. I decided to walk around the building.

The concrete clinic looked even creepier at night. I tiptoed around the side of the building and tried to peek into some windows.

I felt like a cat burglar—or a *dog* burglar, to be exact. Either way, I didn't want to get caught.

I trudged to the back of the building. My eyes lit up when I spotted some cages in a window. I crept closer and peered inside.

I gasped.

It was definitely the right room. Rows of cages lined the room. Water and food bowls sat in the corner of each cage.

But something was wrong. Very wrong.

All the cages were empty.

What happened to the dogs?

And where was Poocher?

I froze when a terrible sound echoed inside the building.

It sounded like a dog's howl.

A howl of pain.

My skin crawled when I heard it again.

It sounded like . . . Poocher.

Someone was hurting him!

7

I banged on the windows of Dr. Diller's Dog Clinic.

"What's going on there?" I screamed. "Let me in! I want to see my dog!"

I ran from window to window. All of them were barred and locked. I dashed to the front door and pushed the buzzer, again and again.

No answer.

"Hello!" I shrieked. "Dr. Diller? It's me! Maggie! Let me in!"

I pounded the huge steel door with my fists.

Nothing. Silence.

Then I heard another sound inside the building. A door slamming.

Somebody was inside. But they were ignoring me!

If Poocher was hurt, I had to help him. How could I help him if I couldn't get inside the clinic?

Mom and Dad were my only hope. I jumped on my bike and zipped home in a panic.

My mind raced even faster than my feet. I kept thinking about Poocher and the sweet way he yipped when he barked.

Then I thought about that awful howl of pain I heard inside the clinic.

What could have happened to Poocher?

I burst through the front door and collapsed in a heap on the living room floor.

Mom and Dad jumped to their feet.

"Maggie, what's wrong?" Dad exclaimed. "What happened?"

"It's Poocher," I panted, catching my breath. "All the dogs are missing, and then I heard Poocher howling. . . . It sounded like he was hurt or something!"

Mom gently pushed the hair out of my eyes. "Maggie, slow down," she urged. "Tell us what happened. Calmly."

I took a deep breath. "I went to see him at Dr. Diller's clinic. I couldn't get in, and then I heard Poocher howling in pain inside," I explained slowly. "I looked in the window, and all the cages were empty. I buzzed the buzzer. I knocked on the door. I pounded on the windows. But nobody would let me in."

Mom glanced up at Dad with a puzzled look on her face.

"I'm sure there's a logical explanation," Dad commented.

"He's right, Maggie," Mom agreed. "Dr. Diller is a very good veterinarian. One of the best. I'm sure Poocher is fine."

"But that awful howling," I argued. "And the empty dog cages. What's going on?"

"There's one way to find out," Mom answered firmly. "I'll call Dr. Diller right now and ask her."

Dad helped me to my feet while Mom dialed the telephone.

Peter appeared at the top of the stairwell. "What's going on?" he asked.

"Nothing, Peter," Dad reported. "We're just making sure Poocher is okay."

"Oh, him." Peter turned and shuffled back to his bedroom.

"Hello, Dr. Diller?" Mom said into the phone. "Hi, this is Mrs. Clark . . . yes, that's right, my daughter is Poocher's owner. I'm calling to see if he's all right."

A pause.

"My daughter dropped by the clinic tonight," Mom continued. "She said she heard a dog howling."

Another pause.

"Yes, I understand," Mom replied. "She also noticed that all the dog cages were empty . . ."

A long pause.

"I see. Thank you, Dr. Diller," Mom went on. "Yes, I know. Maggie's crazy about her new puppy. Yes, tomorrow is fine. Thanks again. Bye."

She hung up the phone.

I was all over Mom in a flash. "What did she say? Is Poocher all right? When can I see him?"

"Poocher is fine," she explained. "Dr. Diller had moved all the dogs to the basement for their special training classes. That's why she couldn't hear the buzzer."

"But what about the howling?" I demanded.

"One of the dogs hurt its leg, but it wasn't Poocher," she assured me. "In fact, we can pick up Poocher tomorrow."

Tomorrow? Yes!

As far as I was concerned, it couldn't come soon enough!

All day Friday, I couldn't wait for school to end. Science class was the worst. Mr. Gosling droned on and on, but I couldn't pay attention. I kept thinking about Poocher.

Finally the bell rang. I dashed out of class.

"Hey, Maggie!" Judy shouted after me. "Want to go to Pete's Pizza? I'm starved!"

I grabbed my books from my locker. "Sorry," I answered quickly. "My mom's picking me up in the car. We're bringing Poocher home today!"

Judy grinned. "Give him a kiss for me, will you?"

"Sure. Later!" I replied, dashing out of the school.

Mom's car was right out front. I hopped inside. "Let's go!"

Mom glanced at me. "Let me guess," she remarked. "You're excited."

The ride across town seemed to last even longer than science class. As soon as Mom parked the car, I jumped out and marched up to the front door of the clinic. I buzzed the buzzer.

The heavy steel door swung open.

"Maggie! Mrs. Clark! Won't you come in?" Dr. Diller greeted us with a smile. "Poocher can't wait to see you."

"How is he?" I asked quickly. "Are you sure he's okay?"

"He's just fine, Maggie," she assured me. "He's even grown since you've seen him. Wait right here. I'll get him."

She turned and passed through a steel doorway. My heart raced when I heard the sound of dogs barking. I tried to listen for Poocher's little yip. But I couldn't hear it.

Finally the door in the hallway swung open. Dr. Diller appeared with a dog on a leash.

"Here's Poocher," she announced cheerfully.

I wanted to jump for joy.

But I couldn't.

Something was wrong.

I stared down at the dog on the leash.

He was bigger than the Poocher I remembered. Much bigger. His fur was darker, and kind of bristly. He seemed . . . different.

"That's Poocher?" I blurted out.

"Oh, Maggie, of course it is!" Mom exclaimed. "He's just grown up a little. Puppies grow very quickly, don't they, Dr. Diller?"

"Very quickly," Dr. Diller agreed.

I gazed down at the strange dog on the leash.

"Poocher?" I said.

The dog jumped up and barked.

And when I say barked, I mean he really *barked!*

A deep, booming woof.

"What happened to his little yip?" I asked Dr. Diller.

The vet grinned again. "His voice changed," she explained. "That little puppy voice doesn't last long. It means only that he's healthy and growing. Here, let me show you all the things Poocher has learned."

Dr. Diller pulled gently on the leash.

"Sit, Poocher," she ordered.

The dog sat.

"Beg, Poocher," she commanded.

The dog lifted his front paws in the air and begged.

"Heel, Poocher. Heel," she said, taking a few steps away.

The dog stood up and trotted obediently to her side.

Then Dr. Diller handed the leash to me. "Here, Maggie, you can try it now," she offered.

"Sit, Poocher," I ordered softly.

The dog sat down.

"Lie down and roll over," I commanded.

He lay down and rolled over.

How cute! I thought. Poocher's a fast learner.

And a fast grower too.

He was already almost as big as Bullhead.

In one week!

"I've written up some instructions for you and your mother, Maggie," Dr. Diller said. "But the most important is to feed Poocher only my special formula dog food. Nothing else. Or he could get very sick."

"Okay." Maybe Dr. Diller's special diet made him grow so fast, I thought.

"Good. Now, why don't you take Poocher outside while your mother signs some papers?" Dr. Diller suggested. "And I'll get your supply of food."

I stared down at the dog. He gazed up at me with big brown eyes.

Those were Poocher's eyes all right. He *was* my Poocher.

But, boy, had he changed.

"Come on, Poocher." I tugged the leash. "Let's go outside."

The dog jumped up and down. I opened the heavy steel door and led him outside.

He sniffed at the air and woofed. Then he tugged on the leash. He pulled me toward our car. I tried to slow down, but he was so strong, I couldn't help running!

Poocher barked and tapped his front paws against the car door. I opened the door.

He leapt inside. I scrambled in after him.

Poocher settled in next to me on the front seat. I stroked his fur.

It was so bristly.
He licked my face with his long tongue.
It felt so scratchy.
I turned and gazed at him.
Poocher stared back at me. . . .
With red, glowing, evil eyes!

8

My breath caught in my throat. I shrank back from Poocher and pressed against the car door. I squeezed my eyes shut.

Those horrible, evil red eyes!

What was he going to do to me?

I sat there, frozen for a moment.

Nothing happened.

Cautiously I opened my eyes. I peeked at Poocher.

His eyes weren't glowing at all!

They were big and brown and sweet. He stared fondly at me. He licked my face again.

I let out a long, shaky breath. It was the sunlight, I told myself. The sunlight must have caught Poocher's eyes at just the right angle.

Either that—or I was starting to see things.

On the drive home, Poocher stuck his head out the window, just like before. His ears flopped in the wind. He barked at passing traffic.

I couldn't help giggling. "That's my Poocher," I cooed, patting his head.

Mom steered the car onto Fear Street. We drove past Billy's house. Bullhead sat quietly in the yard.

But then the ugly bulldog spotted me. He jumped to his feet and charged toward the car.

Poocher stuck his head out the window and barked once.

"Woof!"

Bullhead froze in his tracks.

I couldn't believe it.

Bullhead actually seemed afraid of Poocher!

Cool! Dr. Diller must have taught Poocher how to act tough.

Maybe she could teach me too. Then I wouldn't have to worry about Bullhead or Billy the Bully ever again.

"Welcome home, Poocher," Mom announced as she pulled the car into the driveway.

I opened the car door and Poocher bounded out. He galloped across the yard and leapt onto the front porch. He stood there wagging his tail as Mom opened the door.

Poocher dashed inside. He tackled Peter onto the blue rug in the foyer.

"Whoa, doggy!" Peter shouted.

Poocher barked, deep and low.

"Poocher? Is that you?" Peter asked. "What happened to your funny little yip?"

"Dr. Diller said he grew out of his puppy voice," I explained.

Peter studied the dog. "Wow. How did he get so big so fast?"

"Puppies grow very quickly." I repeated the doctor's answer.

Peter shrugged. "I guess," he replied. "So, Maggie, are you ready to play the super ultimate championship round of Alien Death Squad?"

Boy, did my little brother have a one-track mind. "Not right now," I told him. "I want to spend some time with Poocher."

Peter's face fell. "Oh, all right," he mumbled. He turned and headed for the living room.

I felt a little bad for him. But what did he expect? I hadn't seen Poocher for a week!

I crouched down in front of Poocher. "Are you hungry, boy?" I asked.

Poocher barked. His voice was so deep and low, he sounded like a wild animal in one of those nature movies. Or a monster in a horror film.

It sent a shiver up my spine.

Get used to it, I told myself. This is what he sounds like.

"Come on, boy! Let's go eat!" I said.

Poocher barked again and followed me to the kitchen. I pushed open the swinging kitchen door. Poocher's toenails clicked so loudly on the yellow tiles, I wondered if he had grown claws!

"Dinner coming up!" I announced. I opened the big bag of special food Dr. Diller gave me. I poured a heap into a bowl. "Here you go, Poocher."

Poocher attacked the food like a wild beast.

I couldn't believe how fast he ate it! He gobbled the whole bowl in two bites! Then he licked his chops and gazed up at me.

He wanted more!

"Well, okay, just a little bit more," I agreed.

Poocher wagged his tail as I poured him more food. He buried his nose in the bowl. He scarfed it up in seconds!

"Wow! You never ate that much before," I remarked. "No wonder you got so big!"

I stroked his furry belly. His hair was so bristly, it felt almost pointy. Like porcupine quills.

"Ouch!" I cried. One of Poocher's hairs poked me! I glanced down and gasped.

A tiny drop of blood glistened on my finger.

"Boy, do you need hair conditioner," I commented.

I heard Peter laugh in the living room.

Poocher heard him too. His ears cocked. He barked and pushed through the swinging door.

"Poocher, wait!" I cried.

Too late. Poocher was off and running.
I heard Peter yell in the living room.
Poocher barked.
Something crashed.
"No, Poocher, noooo!" Peter shrieked.

9

I ran into the living room. Mom was right behind me. We both gasped when we saw the mess.

"Bad dog, bad!" Peter scolded.

Mom's favorite flower vase lay shattered on the floor. My little brother picked up the broken pieces. Poocher stood with his tail between his legs.

"My vase!" Mom exclaimed. "It's destroyed!"

Peter pointed at Poocher with a broken piece of the vase. "I tried to stop him," he declared. "He just wouldn't listen."

I felt terrible. Poocher was my dog, so I felt responsible. "Maybe I can glue it together," I offered.

Mom pulled a broom and dustbin out of the closet. "Don't bother, Maggie," she told me. "It's ruined."

Mom swept up the broken pieces.

"I'm sorry," I apologized. "Poocher got away from me."

Mom sighed. "It's all right," she said. "I guess Poocher is still a little clumsy. He's only a puppy."

I nodded and glanced down at Poocher.

My throat closed. I swear I saw a flash of red in his eyes. A glowing glint of evil.

But when I looked again, his eyes were normal.

Oh, no. Was there something wrong with my dog?

Or was there something wrong with *me?*

The rest of the evening passed quietly. Poocher padded around the house, sniffing into corners and exploring.

I still couldn't get over how much he had changed.

"Come on, Poocher, bedtime," I called at last.

Poocher bounded into the kitchen. I opened the back door and pointed at his doghouse. "Okay, Poocher. Go to sleep now."

Poocher glanced at the doghouse, then up at me, whining.

"Go on, boy," I ordered. "Go to sleep."

Poocher's tail dropped between his legs. He lowered his head and walked slowly to the doghouse.

"Sweet dreams, puppy," I called, and closed the door.

When Poocher first arrived, I planned to beg Mom and Dad to let him sleep in my room. But now that he was so big and strong, I sort of didn't mind him sleeping in his own little house.

I went upstairs and changed into my nightgown.

A long, eerie howl echoed in the backyard.

Poocher? I wondered. Is that you?

I pulled aside a corner of the curtain and peeked out my bedroom window. Moonlight shone on the dark lawn and made the picket fence glow silver.

Poocher sat in front of his doghouse. He tilted back his head and bayed at the moon.

Such a strange, creepy sound! It made me shiver.

Then Poocher turned his head and stared right at my window.

Was he looking at me? Did he know I was there?

What was he thinking?

I dropped the curtain and stepped back. My hands were shaking. Don't be silly, I told myself. He's only a puppy.

I reached for Bilbo, my teddy bear. I hugged him tightly. I know it's silly to hug a teddy bear when you're twelve years old. But I got Bilbo when I was three. I couldn't stand the thought of giving him up.

If Judy or anyone else at school knew about Bilbo, I'd die of embarrassment. But right now it felt good to hold him.

I placed Bilbo next to my pillow. Then I reached for my robe and slippers. Maybe a snack would make me feel better.

Another eerie howl echoed in the backyard.

I shuddered again. Poocher's voice gave me the creeps.

I pulled on my robe. Then I slipped my left foot into

a slipper. Something cold and slimy squished against my toes.

"Gross!" I muttered. Quickly I pulled my foot out of the slipper. I held it up and peered inside.

Inside the slipper was a mouse.

A dead mouse.

And its head was completely torn off its body!

10

I screamed and leapt backward, dropping the slipper.
How did a dead mouse get in there?
And what happened to its head?
Then it hit me.
Poocher!
Poocher killed the mouse! Poocher tore its head off!
Who else could it be?
I shuddered. How could Poocher do such a thing? It was horrible!
I jumped when my bedroom door swung open.
"What's wrong?" Peter asked. "I heard you scream."
I pointed at the slipper on the floor.
Peter crouched down and peered into the slipper.

"Looks like Poocher killed a mouse," he stated calmly.

"But he's only a puppy!" I wailed. "How could he do something so . . . so . . . gross?"

Peter shrugged. "He's an animal. Animals kill things."

"Not Poocher," I insisted.

"He's got teeth and claws," Peter went on. "And he already broke Mom's vase. Face it, Maggie. Poocher is a bad dog."

"Shut up!" I yelled.

It would be terrible if Peter was right!

Dad burst into the room. "What's all the shouting about?"

Peter grabbed Dad by the arm and pointed to the slipper. "Look what Poocher did!" he blurted out. "He killed a mouse! He ripped its head off!"

Dad squatted down and peered into the slipper. He reached inside. And pulled the mouse out by the tail!

"Take it away!" I shrieked.

Dad squeezed the mouse.

It squeaked.

"It's just a rubber chew toy," Dad explained.

Peter burst out laughing. He grabbed the rubber mouse and squeezed. "It sure scared Maggie!" he whooped. "A rubber mouse! Ha! Poocher mangled it! What a bad dog!"

My face turned red. "Get out of here now, Peter," I snapped. "Leave me alone. Good night!"

Peter swung the rubber mouse by the tail. He sauntered out of the room, laughing.

Dad looked at me and shrugged. "At least it wasn't a real mouse, Maggie," he said, trying to console me.

It didn't work. I felt like such a geek.

Dad said good night and left the room. I decided to skip brushing my teeth and just go to bed. I crawled under the covers.

Bilbo stared at me with his blue button eyes. At least *he* didn't make fun of me.

Was Peter right? Was Poocher a bad dog?

And why did Poocher make me so nervous?

I sighed. Getting a dog was supposed to solve all my problems.

Instead, Poocher was giving me a whole set of new ones.

Saturday morning I woke up feeling great.

The sun was shining. Birds were chirping. Last night seemed like nothing but a bad dream. It was the perfect day to take Poocher to the park!

I dressed in a hurry and rushed down the stairs.

Mom and Peter sat at the kitchen table. Dad served them eggs and bacon and pancakes. It's the only thing he can cook, so he always treats us every weekend.

"Good morning, sleepyhead," Dad greeted me with a smile.

"Morning," I replied cheerfully. "Is Poocher in the house?"

Mom glanced up from her plate. "He's been using the doggy door all morning long," she said with amusement. "Coming and going, going and coming. What a busy dog!"

I laughed. "Where is he now?"

"Backyard," Peter answered through a mouthful of pancakes.

I headed for the back door.

"Wait, Maggie," Dad called. "I'll fix a plate of pancakes for you if you run out front and grab the morning paper."

"I thought Poocher was supposed to fetch the paper," Peter pointed out.

"We'll have to teach him," Dad remarked. "But for now, we have Maggie. Fetch, Maggie, fetch!"

"Ha-ha-ha," I groaned.

I strolled to the front door and stepped onto the porch.

What a great day! Poocher was going to love the park!

I went down the walk and opened the gate. The newspaper was stuffed in the mailbox. I reached for it.

"Hey, Maggie! Where's Poocher?" a voice called.

I spun around. Billy the Bully stood ten feet away. By his side, Bullhead growled and tugged on a leash.

"Get lost!" I snapped. "Or else . . ."

"Or else what?" Billy scoffed. "You'll sic Poocher on us?"

"That's right. Poocher!" I yelled. "Here, boy!"

No Poocher. No huge dog bounding to my rescue.

Grinning, Billy let go of Bullhead's leash.

Bullhead charged right at me!

I shrieked. And scrambled on top of our white picket fence.

I shoved my feet between the slats and clutched the

pointy tips. I must have looked really stupid with my rear end sticking way up in the air.

Billy burst out laughing. "No wonder Bullhead is always going after you. You look like a dumb cat up there."

Bullhead snapped at my feet.

"Make him stop!" I screamed. "Billy!"

I couldn't believe it. I was trapped on top of the fence! Any second I was going to snap my ankle or fall over.

If I didn't die of embarrassment first.

Billy snorted. "I'll make a deal, Maggie," he told me. "Bullhead and I will leave you alone—if you do my homework."

"No way!" I yelled. "Go away!"

Bullhead barked at me. I clung to the fence. "Make him stop, Billy," I shouted. "I'm serious."

Billy let me wait for a full minute. Finally he snapped his fingers. "Down, boy, down!" he ordered. "That's enough. For now."

Bullhead trotted to Billy's side.

"See you, Maggie," Billy said. "Unless you see us first, of course." They took off down the street.

I slid down from the fence and collapsed on the ground.

"Poocher!" I groaned. Where was my puppy when I needed him?

I stormed into the house with the newspaper. I slapped it down on the kitchen table and wolfed down my breakfast.

Mom and Dad stared at me curiously.

"Is something wrong?" Mom asked me.

I didn't want to tell them about Billy and Bullhead. So I just shook my head. "I'm in a hurry," I explained. "I want to take Poocher to the park."

"Have you made your bed yet?" Mom questioned me.

I sighed. "No," I muttered.

"Well, you can take Poocher out *after* you make your bed."

I gulped down a glass of milk. "Oh, all right," I mumbled. I wiped my mouth with a napkin and excused myself.

I dashed upstairs to make my bed. No problem. I was great at making beds. I could do it in thirty seconds flat.

But something was wrong. Something was missing.

Where was Bilbo?

I searched under the covers, under the pillows, under the bed—everywhere.

No teddy bear.

Where could I have put him?

I went downstairs to question Peter. He sat in front of the television playing Alien Death Squad. Again.

"Have you seen Bilbo?" I asked.

"Your stupid teddy bear?" Peter grumbled. "No, leave me alone. I'm just about to crush the alien headquarters."

Bilbo had to be somewhere in the house. I remembered falling asleep with him right next to me. How far could he have gone?

I'll find him later, I decided. Time for the park.

I grabbed Poocher's leash and hurried into the backyard.

As I passed by the picnic table, I noticed something sticking out of the ground. Something furry. I took a step closer and peered at the fuzzy brown object.

It was Bilbo's paw.

11

Someone buried my teddy bear!

His little brown arm stuck out of the freshly dug earth. I couldn't see the rest of him. His whole body must be buried underground.

I crouched down for a closer look. Yes, it was Bilbo's arm. I'd recognize that furry little paw anywhere!

My heart raced. Frantically, I started digging. I pulled the furry arm gently. It popped up in my hand.

Just the arm!

Someone tore his arm off his body!

I stood up. I scanned the yard. It was spotted with little mounds of dirt. And pieces of Bilbo!

My stomach churned. Who would do this horrible thing to my teddy bear?

Maybe Billy and his stupid dog Bullhead were mean enough to do it. But they couldn't have gotten into the house.

No. It wasn't Billy and Bullhead.

Peter's words echoed in my head.

He's a bad dog. A bad dog.

Poocher!

Poocher must have destroyed Bilbo. Pulled him off my bed. Ripped him apart with his teeth and claws. Shredded him to pieces. And buried him in the yard.

It was horrible. But it was the only answer that made sense.

Only—why?

Was Poocher jealous of my teddy bear?

Or was he just playing?

I gazed around the lawn. Poor Bilbo! My childhood teddy bear! My best friend since I was a baby! Now look at him!

Slowly I gathered the pieces together. The teddy bear arms, teddy bear legs, teddy bear body . . .

Where was Bilbo's head?

I had a bad feeling. Slowly, I turned toward the doghouse.

Poocher lay in the doorway. His head was lowered. He was chewing something.

I tiptoed closer.

"Poocher?" I whispered.

Poocher raised his head and stared at me.

Clenched between his paws was Bilbo's head.

Poocher licked his chops and gnawed hungrily on the chewed-up head of my teddy bear.

Bilbo's face was shredded to bits!

It was horrible.

"Poocher? How could you?" I wailed.

I had to save what was left of poor Bilbo. I reached down between Poocher's paws for Bilbo's head.

Poocher growled at me. His lip quivered and curled back from his long, gleaming fangs.

I froze. The hair rose up on my arms. An icy chill swept through my body.

My own dog was eating my teddy bear's head.

And now he seemed ready to attack me.

What kind of horrible monster was Poocher?

12

Poocher and I gazed at each other. But now I was more mad than afraid. I had to get Bilbo's head away from Poocher.

"Easy, Poocher," I muttered.

He stopped growling and cocked his ears. His tail thumped on the floor of his doghouse.

So far so good. Cautiously, I patted his head with my left hand. He licked it.

Then I grabbed Bilbo's head with my right hand.

Poocher leapt up and barked. He wanted Bilbo's head back!

But I wasn't going to give it to him. No way!

I turned and fled toward the house. I flung open the kitchen door and ran inside.

Poocher tried to follow me. I slammed the back door in his face. I was so mad at him!

And so scared.

The door didn't stop Poocher, of course. He simply hurtled through the doggy door. Mom and Dad glanced up at us from the kitchen table.

"Mom! Dad! Look what Poocher did to Bilbo!" I cried. I tossed Bilbo's head onto the kitchen table. "He ripped him up and buried him all over the yard!"

The kitchen door swung open and Peter entered the room. His eyes lit up when he saw Bilbo's head.

"I told you!" he exclaimed. "Poocher is a bad dog!"

"Shut up, Peter," I snapped. I didn't need his annoying comments right now.

Mom put her arm around my shoulder. "I'm sorry about Bilbo, honey. But you have to remember that Poocher is only a puppy. Puppies like to chew things up and bury them."

Dad nodded. "That's right," he agreed. "You have to be more careful with your things now that we have a dog in the house."

I flung myself into a chair. "I know, but . . ." I trailed off and glanced around the kitchen.

Poocher was gone. He must have wandered into the living room.

"But what?" Mom prodded.

I took a deep breath. "I know this is going to sound crazy," I began. I lowered my voice. "But I think something is wrong with Poocher."

"Don't be ridiculous, Maggie," Mom said, laughing. "Poocher is a perfectly normal, frisky puppy."

"Maybe we should send him back to Dr. Diller," Dad suggested. "Maybe he needs a little more training."

"Dr. Diller can't change him," Peter objected. "He's a bad dog, through and through."

"Now, Peter," Mom said. "We all have to get used to the fact that we're living with a baby animal here."

She turned to me. "Right, Maggie?"

"I guess," I agreed reluctantly.

But why did I feel as if I were living with a monster?

That night I crawled into bed without my teddy bear.

I missed Bilbo already. How could Poocher do such a thing?

I sighed. Maybe Mom and Dad were right. I shouldn't blame Poocher. I should have placed Bilbo on a high shelf, out of Poocher's reach. He didn't know any better.

Yawning, I slid under the sheets and turned out the light. I closed my eyes.

And bolted upright as a long, eerie howl echoed in the yard.

My body tensed as I listened. The howl was deep and loud. Could that be Poocher?

No. No *dog* howled like that. It sounded like a creature out of a nightmare.

I crawled out of bed and crept to the window. I peeked through the curtains.

The backyard was dark. The moon hid behind

racing clouds. I could barely make out the picnic table and barbecue below me.

Gradually my eyes adjusted. I spotted Poocher's doghouse in the corner of the yard.

Scratch. Scratch. Scratch.

The sound was like nails on metal. It made the hair prickle on the back of my neck.

And it definitely came from Poocher's doghouse.

I peered into the darkness. Two red points of light glowed inside the doghouse. They looked like . . . eyes.

A giant, clawed paw reached out of the doghouse. Then another. Step by step, something emerged into the moonlight.

My breath caught in my throat.

It was Poocher.

And Poocher was a monster!

I mean, a *real* monster.

He was six feet tall and still growing. His body bristled with sharp quills instead of fur. A weird pinkish glow seemed to surround him in the dark. And his eyes blazed an evil red.

He stared right at me. He licked his fangs.

Huge, glistening fangs.

I couldn't move. I couldn't scream. I watched helplessly as the monster-dog bounded across the yard.

And started climbing straight up the side of the house!

13

Higher and higher Poocher climbed. Right toward my window.

Ka-thunk! His huge paws hit the side of the house hard. *Scraaaatcchhh.* His claws dug into the wood. Then—*skreeeee*—he yanked them out.

Ka-thunk! Scraaaatccchhh! Skreeeee!

"Poocher, no!" I whispered. "This can't be happening!"

I stepped back from the window and shut my eyes. Maybe I was imagining it. Maybe it would stop.

It didn't. The horrible scraping and clawing sounded as if Poocher were tearing the whole house apart.

I opened my eyes and peered out the window.

Poocher clung to the side of the house—only five feet away from me!

And getting closer every second.

What was he going to do to me?

The monster-dog crawled up to the window.

His massive jaws snapped, inches from my face. He raised his huge, clawed foot.

I screamed and threw myself backward.

Thunk! My head hit something hard.

The headboard of my bed.

I stared wildly around.

I was sitting up in bed. Moonlight streamed in through my window. There was no monster there. No hideous, nightmare Poocher.

A dream! It was only a dream. A terrifying nightmare.

Relief flooded through me. It wasn't *real!* I was safe.

My sheets were drenched with sweat. I climbed out of bed and tiptoed to the window. I peered through the pink curtains.

Moonlight silvered the backyard. A bright beam fell upon Poocher's doghouse.

Silence.

No howling. No scratching. No monster-dog in sight.

I was losing it. Totally losing it!

I stood there for a second longer while my heartbeat slowed down. Then I headed back to my bed.

That's when I heard a strange sound.

Scratching.

It came from downstairs.

Something was scratching down there. Just like in my dream!

Was it Poocher? What was he doing in the house? Was he doing something terrible?

Was my dream some kind of warning? Was my dog a monster?

I was afraid to find out what was downstairs. But I had to. I had to know the truth.

I pulled on my robe and slippers. Quietly, I opened my bedroom door. I peered into the hallway.

Nothing. I crept to the top of the stairs and listened.

Scratch. Scratch. Scratch.

That strange sound again! What was it?

Slowly, I tiptoed down the stairs. I held my breath as I reached the first floor.

Scratch. Scratch. Scratch.

The sound was coming from the living room. I crept down the hallway, one nerve-racking step at a time. My heart pounded in my chest.

Carefully, I peeked around the corner.

My heart almost stopped.

"No!" I cried.

14

"Peter!" I gasped. "It's *you!*"

My little brother jumped. Dad's old record collection was scattered across the room. Peter held a kitchen fork in one hand and a record in the other.

He was scratching up Dad's old records!

"What are you doing?" I demanded. "Are you crazy?"

Peter stared down at the floor. He didn't answer.

Why? Why would Peter get up in the middle of the night and scratch up a bunch of records? It didn't make any sense.

Then it hit me.

The rat!

He was going to blame it on Poocher!

I could hear my little brother's voice. "Face it, Maggie. Poocher is just a bad dog."

But maybe it wasn't Poocher at all. Maybe it was Peter!

I glared at him. "You're the one who really broke Mom's vase, aren't you? You were in the room with Poocher. You said it was him. But it was really you, wasn't it?"

Peter glanced up. He still didn't answer. But I could tell by his flushed cheeks that I was right.

"And you ripped up Bilbo and buried him in the yard," I went on. "Then you let me think Poocher did it."

Peter hunched his shoulders. "It was just a dumb teddy bear," he muttered.

"I can't believe you. *You're* the real monster around here!" I cried. "Poor Poocher! I've been blaming him for everything—and it was you all along! How could you do it?"

Peter lowered his head. "I don't like Poocher," he mumbled. "Ever since he came along, it's always Poocher, Poocher, Poocher. You never even play with me anymore. Just Poocher."

"What are you talking about?" I scoffed.

"I had it all figured out," Peter explained. "If I did bad things and made it look like Poocher did them, then you and Mom and Dad wouldn't like Poocher so much. You'd get rid of him, and things would go back to normal."

I opened my mouth. But I didn't know what to say. So I shut it again.

Maybe he was right. Maybe I spent too much time thinking about Poocher. Maybe I should have played that super ultimate championship Alien Death Squad tournament with Peter.

Suddenly I felt sorry for my little brother. Kind of.

I folded my arms. "All right, listen," I said gruffly. "I think what you did stinks. But I won't tell Mom and Dad on you—if you quit picking on Poocher. Deal?"

Peter nodded. "Deal."

"And if you clean up after dinner on my night for the next month," I added quickly.

Peter rolled his eyes. "Okay, okay."

"And—"

"Hey! No fair!" Peter protested.

"Okay, I guess that's enough. But if you don't do it right, I'm telling." I yawned. "Now, clean up this mess. I'm going back to bed."

I climbed the stairs slowly. My whole body felt weak with relief. My Poocher wasn't a monster at all! I felt terrible that I blamed him for everything Peter did.

I'll make it all up to Poocher tomorrow, I decided.

I woke up Monday morning feeling great. Everything was okay now. I couldn't believe that I ever thought Poocher was a monster! I laughed. "What an imagination," I muttered.

I opened my curtains and peered out. Bright sunlight glinted off the leaves in the backyard. Poocher bounded across the lawn, barking at squirrels.

What a cute puppy! I had to be extra nice to him today, I decided. To make up for thinking such horrible things about him.

I pulled on a T-shirt and jeans and hurried downstairs. I gulped down some cereal and juice. Then I dug through the refrigerator. Great! It was still there. A leftover ham bone from last night's dinner.

"Mom, can I give this to Poocher?" I asked.

Mom frowned. "He's not supposed to have anything but Dr. Diller's special formula," she reminded me.

"I know. But I want to give him a special treat."

"Well, I was saving it for soup," Mom began.

"Oh, please?" I begged.

Mom smiled. "Oh, all right. Just this once."

"Thanks!" I cried.

The doorbell rang. "Maggie," Peter called. "Judy's here."

Judy and I usually walk to school together.

"Be right there," I called back.

I dashed out to the backyard. Poocher bounced up to me with his tail wagging.

"Hello, puppy," I crooned. "I'm sorry I ever thought you were a bad dog. In fact, I'm going to give you a treat to make up for all my dumb ideas."

Poocher gazed adoringly at me. He licked my nose.

Yuck! Puppy slobber.

I held out the bone. "Look what I have for you! A great big, juicy bone!"

Poocher's ears perked up. He started to drool.

"Here you go, boy." I tossed the bone onto the grass.

Poocher pounced. He attacked the bone hungrily.

Too bad I have to go to school, I thought. I wish I could play with him all day!

"See you later, Poocher," I called. "Be a good dog!"

When I got home from school that afternoon, I found a note on the little table in the front hall. I picked it up.

"'Dear Maggie and Peter,'" I read. "'Dad and I have to take Grandma and Grandpa to the airport. Home by eight or nine. Microwave pizza in the freezer. Enjoy and be good! Mom.'"

I glanced up as Peter came bouncing down the stairs.

"We're on our own!" he cheered. "Want to throw a party?"

Yeah, right.

"I'm taking Poocher to the park," I told him.

When I saw him frown, I remembered what he said last night. About me never having time for him.

"Um—want to come?" I asked.

Peter's eyes lit up. But he tried to act casual. "Okay," he said, shrugging.

"Great! I'll get Poocher." I grabbed the leash from the hook in the kitchen, then opened the back door.

"Poocher?" I called. I skipped across the lawn.

Poocher lay in his doghouse. I could just see his paws and the tip of his nose poking out. He gnawed happily on something.

How cute, I thought. He's still chewing his ham bone.

As I reached the doghouse, I glanced down at the grass.

Huh? The ham bone lay at my feet.

So what was Poocher chewing on?

I bent down for a closer look.

"Oh, no!" I gasped. *"No!"*

Resting between Poocher's paws was a skull.

A *human* skull!

15

A human skull! How in the world did Poocher get hold of it?

I slapped my hand over my mouth to hold in a scream.

Poocher stopped chewing.

The skull fell from his mouth. It rolled across the grass.

Poocher fixed his eyes upon me. They glowed red.

Bright, evil red.

I pinched myself. Ow!

This was no nightmare. This was real!

I took another step backward. My heart pounded in my chest. I started to tremble.

Poocher growled and took a step toward me!

I didn't dare scream. Not when Poocher stared at me with those wild red eyes.

He barked. The deep sound echoed across the yard.

His tongue lolled out of his mouth as he stared at me, panting.

Yikes! His teeth! They were so long!

And his claws. They looked like knives!

And his fur. It bristled out around him like a porcupine's quills!

I couldn't believe it. This wasn't the Poocher I knew and loved.

This was the monster-dog from my nightmare!

I took another step back and glanced around desperately. I spotted a stick on the ground.

It was my only chance.

I reached down and grabbed the stick. I waved it in the air in front of Poocher.

Poocher sniffed the stick. His nostrils flared.

"Fetch, Poocher, f-fetch!" I stammered weakly.

I tossed the stick over the picket fence.

Poocher turned his huge head and followed the stick with his eyes. But he didn't chase it.

He turned back to me.

His eyes blazed red. His fangs glistened.

He didn't want the stupid stick.

He wanted me!

"No, Poocher!" I cried.

Poocher tilted back his head and howled. The horrible sound made my skin crawl. Then he did something that was worse. Much, much worse.

He stood up on his back legs like a human being.

And he started walking toward me!

Clump! Clump! He stalked across the grass. His front paws hung down in front of his chest. The long claws glistened.

Poocher isn't a dog at all, I thought in horror. He's really, truly a monster!

Poocher circled around me. He crouched down on all fours. I stared at him in terror. I wanted to scream. But it was as if I had a golf ball stuck in my throat.

Then he pounced!

I ducked and spun away. Poocher landed on the ground behind me. He barked and turned around. He stared at me.

He was going to attack again!

I bolted for the house.

Poocher galloped past me. He circled around in front, reared up, and raised his claws.

I shrieked and dove under the picnic table.

Poocher leapt through the air. He landed on top of the table with a heavy thud. His heavy tail beat against the wood. *Thump! Thump! Thump!*

It was so weird—almost as if Poocher were playing cat and mouse with me. Does he think this is a game? I wondered desperately.

Scrrrrrrrrkkk! Something tore right through the boards of the table.

A long, gleaming claw slashed inches from my face!

I screamed.

If this was a game, I didn't want to be the loser!

I scrambled backward. My foot bumped into something.

It was one of the rubber snakes from Peter's birthday gift. I picked it up and tossed it into the yard.

Poocher pounced on the toy snake. And I dashed toward the house!

I caught sight of Peter, peering out through the kitchen window. I guess he was wondering where we were. When he spotted Poocher, a look of horror flashed across his face.

I staggered toward the back door and grabbed the knob.

Locked!

"Peter!" I screamed. "Let me in! Hurry! Peter!"

I glanced over my shoulder. Uh-oh.

Poocher had torn the toy snake in two. And now he was coming after me again!

I shrieked in fear as Poocher charged toward me. I twisted the doorknob and pushed hard.

Still locked!

I heard Peter inside, fumbling with the bolt.

"Peter! Hurry!" I hollered.

Poocher barked. I glanced back in horror. His red eyes flashed wickedly at me. My whole body trembled.

Then Poocher leapt!

"Nooooo!" I yelled. I shut my eyes—and tumbled into the kitchen.

Yes! Peter had opened the door just in time.

He slammed it in Poocher's face. Poocher crashed

against the back door with a loud crunch. He yelped angrily.

I jumped to my feet. "Peter! You saved me!" I panted. I clutched his arm.

My little brother's eyes bugged out. "What's going on?" he cried in terror. "What is that . . . that . . . thing?"

"It's Poocher!" I yelled. "He's a monster, Peter. A real monster!"

We both jumped as the door rattled. Poocher's claw scraped against the wood. I hoped he couldn't break through it the way he broke through the picnic table.

Then I realized he didn't have to break through.

"The doggy door!" I cried. "We have to block—"

Too late.

The doggy door swung open.

A furry claw burst through.

Poocher was coming in!

16

Peter and I screamed.

The doggy door swung open farther. Another clawed foot shot through. Then a long, hairy snout.

"Run!" Peter shrieked.

But there wasn't time to run.

Poocher burst through the doggy door!

His claws scraped the linoleum as he spun around. He snarled and reared up on his hind legs. Peter and I stared in horror.

Poocher sure had changed. His puppy body was bulked up with big, bulging muscles. His nose looked pointier and his teeth were definitely longer—much longer. And his fur stood up so thick and wild, it made him look like a giant pincushion.

Still, I could tell it was Poocher.

Even when he roared at us.

Peter and I scrambled across the floor. We crawled beneath the table and pushed the chairs in front of us.

Poocher hopped up on one of the chairs and howled. The sound was piercing. I clamped my hands over my ears.

Poocher suddenly stopped howling. I risked a peek out from under the table.

He was tilting his head the way dogs do when they hear something.

"What is he doing?" Peter whispered.

"Shhh," I replied. I put a finger to my lips. We all strained to hear.

Bleep . . . bleep . . . bleep!

The weird sound echoed faintly from the living room.

"It's Alien Death Squad," Peter whispered. "I left the game on."

"Shhh," I hushed him. "Don't move."

Poocher turned his head toward the sound. Slowly, he stepped off the chair and padded toward the doorway. He peered curiously into the hallway.

"Now's our chance, Peter," I whispered. "Run for it!"

We dashed toward the back door.

Too late.

Poocher charged after us, barking fiercely.

I staggered backward—and bumped into the pantry door.

"In here, Peter!" I cried. "Quick!"

Peter flung open the pantry door. We dove inside. Peter slammed the door shut.

Poocher clawed at the other side. He barked wildly. And clawed some more.

"Go away, Poocher!" I shouted through the door. "Go away, boy! Bad dog! Bad!"

But my yells only made him try harder to get in.

I slumped down on the floor of the pantry.

Poocher scratched and scratched at the door.

"Me and my great ideas," I muttered. "Now we're trapped!"

17

Skreee! Skreee! Skreee!

Poocher's claws scraped down the pantry door.

I sat down on a jumbo-sized box of instant mashed potatoes. Peter plopped down on a stepladder. And we waited.

And waited.

And waited.

Skreee! Skreee! Skreee!

"How long are we going to be trapped in here?" Peter whispered. "Isn't Poocher going to get tired?"

"I don't think monsters get tired," I replied.

"You really think he's a monster? I mean, a *real* monster?"

I snorted. "What do *you* think? You saw him. How many normal dogs do you know whose claws are a foot long and who walk on their hind legs? And do you know what he was gnawing on? A human skull! He must have dug it up from the Fear Street Cemetery. How many normal dogs do you know who dig up bones from cemeteries? And how many normal dogs—"

"Okay, okay," Peter interrupted. "Forget I asked. You're right." He shivered. "He's definitely a monster."

We sat there glumly for a minute.

Skreee! Skreee! Skreee!

Peter folded his arms and frowned. "So how do you think it happened? How did he turn into a monster?"

"I don't know," I groaned. "I'm so confused! When we first brought him home from Dr. Diller's Dog Clinic, I thought there was something wrong with him. He looked so different. Then he did all those terrible things. . . ."

"But that was really me playing a joke," Peter said.

"Right." I punched his arm. "Which made me think Poocher was fine and *you* were the monster."

"Thanks a lot," Peter huffed.

"Well, it's true!" I snapped. "You had me so freaked out about Poocher that I even had a terrible nightmare about him."

Skreee! Skreee! Skreee! Poocher's claws scraped on the pantry door.

"That's no dream," Peter murmured.

"I know," I groaned.

Skreee! Skreee! Skreee!

"I felt so terrible about thinking Poocher was a

monster that I gave him a special treat before school this morning," I said sadly. "But when I came home . . ." I shuddered.

Peter stared at me. "You gave him something special to eat?"

I nodded. "A ham bone."

"Didn't Dr. Diller say you couldn't feed Poocher anything but her special food?" Peter demanded. "Mom gave me a whole lecture about it when you guys came home from the clinic."

My eyes widened. "You're right!" I gasped. "Oh, no! Maybe I made Poocher sick by giving him the bone."

My mind reeled. "This is terrible. It's *my* fault Poocher is like this!"

Peter shook his head. "I don't know. Don't you think it would take more than the wrong food to turn a puppy into a monster?"

I bit my lip. I was sure I was right. Something about switching his food must have transformed Poocher into the horrible, mutated *thing* outside.

But then I thought of something.

"Hey! Mom said Dr. Diller is a brilliant veterinarian," I said excitedly. "One of the best in the country. What if we take Poocher to Dr. Diller's clinic? Maybe she can cure him!"

Peter shook his head firmly. "No way," he declared. "It's him or us, Maggie. We have to find a way to destroy Poocher!"

"How can you say that?" I wailed. "It isn't his fault he's the way he is. What if there's a cure? I know Dr. Diller will help us!"

"Okay. Let's say Dr. Diller can help Poocher. There's still one big problem," Peter told me.

"What?" I asked impatiently.

"We have to get out of here first!"

Duh. How could I forget?

Groaning, I slumped back onto the huge box of instant mashed potatoes.

We were stuck.

Then Peter's eyes lit up. "Maggie!" he whispered. "Listen!"

I sat still and listened.

"What?" I asked. "I don't hear anything."

"That's right!" Peter exclaimed. *"No scratching!"*

My jaw dropped.

Peter was right! Poocher wasn't scratching the door anymore!

"Maybe he decided to leave us alone," Peter whispered. "Maybe he got bored and went outside."

"Or maybe he's waiting for us right outside the door," I pointed out.

Peter and I stared at each other.

"There's only one way to find out," I said grimly.

Peter nodded. "I know. But I'm scared."

"Me too," I agreed.

I stood up. I reached for the handle of the pantry door. Peter jumped up and positioned himself next to me.

"Okay," I whispered. "Ready. Set. Go."

I opened the pantry door an inch. I peered out.

No Poocher.

"The coast is clear," I murmured.

I pushed the door open a little farther. And a little farther.

Still no Poocher in sight.

Peter and I tiptoed into the kitchen. I trembled with each step. We stopped and scanned the room.

"We're safe," Peter whispered. "Poocher must have— *Maggie! Look out!*"

18

I spun around just as Poocher burst out from behind the pantry door.

He swiped the air with his claws. His fur stood up on end. He barked. No, he roared.

Then he lunged.

I screamed and ducked.

Peter yanked me back into the pantry. *Slam!*

Peter leaned against the pantry door. We were safe again.

And trapped again.

Poocher snarled outside the pantry. He scratched the door even harder than before. *Skreeeee! Skreeeee! Skreeeee!*

"We better rethink this Dr. Diller idea," Peter muttered.

I didn't want to give up. "Maybe he's just hungry," I suggested. "Maybe we should feed him."

I squinted around, inspecting the pantry.

"Look! There's a big bag of Dr. Diller's Doggy Snacks." I pointed. "On top of the dog carrier."

"Dog carrier?" Peter asked. "Is that what this thing is?"

He moved the bag of Doggy Snacks and studied the carrier. It was a big yellow plastic box with a wire door and air holes on the sides. I pulled it out to the middle of the pantry floor.

"See? You put your dog in it when you travel," I explained.

Peter opened the door latch and peeked inside.

"It's huge," he observed.

"I know," I agreed. "Dad complained that it was too big for Poocher, but Mom said he would grow."

The pantry door rattled as Poocher threw himself against it.

"Mom was right," Peter muttered, shivering. "Poocher did grow. A lot."

I slumped down on top of the dog carrier. "If only we could get him in here somehow . . . But how?"

"What happened to feeding him?" Peter wanted to know.

I gasped and jumped up. "Peter! You're brilliant!"

He stared. "I am?"

"Yes! Don't you see?" I cried. "We can lure Poocher into the dog carrier with these Doggy Snacks! Then we put the carrier on your red wagon and take Poocher to Dr. Diller!"

Peter's face lit up. "I *am* brilliant!" he agreed.

Quickly, we made our plans.

Peter positioned the dog carrier in front of the pantry door. He opened the latch door and crouched down behind it. I placed some Doggy Snacks in the carrier.

Then I slipped a Doggy Snack beneath the pantry door.

We heard Poocher sniff at the food.

Crunch! Gulp!

"Yes!" I pumped my fist in the air. "He's eating!"

I slipped another Doggy Snack under the door. Then another. And another.

Poocher gobbled them up. I could hear him slobbering. It sounded like he was starving.

My heart filled with hope. Maybe Poocher wasn't trying to hurt us at all. Maybe he was just hungry. Maybe this was how a monster dog begged for food!

I poked another snack beneath the door, then quickly pulled it back.

Poocher barked and scratched at the door.

I did it again.

Poocher's tongue slipped beneath the door.

"Get ready, Peter!" I whispered. "On three."

I teased Poocher once again with a Doggy Snack.

He barked.

"One. Two. Three!" I cried—and flung open the door.

Poocher burst into the pantry.

And plunged headfirst into the dog carrier!

His huge, bristly body moved so fast, I could barely see it. But I heard the thud when his head hit the side of the carrier.

Wham! Peter slammed the door and latched it.

It worked!

Poocher was trapped!

"Yes!" I whooped. "We did it, Peter! We did it! All right!"

Peter and I cheered and jumped up and down.

A strange sound stopped us. Silence.

Peter peered into the dog carrier. "Whoa. Poocher is out cold!" he exclaimed.

I leaned down and peeked into the air holes of the box. Peter was right. Poocher was zonked.

"I hope he didn't hit his head too hard," I said, worried.

I watched Poocher's belly rise and fall. His eyes didn't glow now—they were shut tight.

He was in doggy dreamland.

"Poor Poocher," I whispered softly. "We have to help you."

"We better get him to Dr. Diller's before he wakes up," Peter pointed out. "I don't think I want to be around him when he's *really* mad."

"You're right." I glanced at the dog carrier nervously. "Go get your wagon from the garage, Peter. And hurry!"

* * *

We rolled Peter's wagon up to the front door of Dr. Diller's Dog Clinic. The whole building was dark. Moonlight gleamed in the barred windows.

"This place looks really creepy," Peter muttered.

"I know," I agreed. "But Dr. Diller is the only one who can help Poocher."

I stared at Poocher through the wire door of his carrier.

Poor puppy! He couldn't help it if he was a monster. Something was wrong with him. Terribly wrong.

And it might be all my fault!

Dr. Diller *had* to help us.

I climbed the steps and pressed the buzzer next to the door.

No one answered.

I tried not to freak out. Dr. Diller was probably working in the basement and couldn't hear the buzzer. Like the last time I visited after hours.

"There's got to be a way to get inside," I muttered.

Peter reached over and rattled the door handle.

The door swung open.

He grinned at me. "Aren't you glad I'm so brilliant?"

"Oh, shut up," I snapped.

We left Poocher outside in his carrier. No way could we carry him up all those steps!

I moved inside. "Dr. Diller?" I called.

No answer. Our footsteps echoed in the dark, empty hallway. I turned to Peter. "She's probably in the basement, doing that special training stuff she does. Let's check it out."

We came to a door that was open a crack. I pulled it wide and saw a set of stairs leading down to the basement. A dim reddish glow came up the stairs.

"We're not going down there, are we?" Peter asked, his voice trembling. "It's creepy."

I gazed into the eerie glow.

It *was* creepy. And it was so quiet.

Was Dr. Diller even down there?

I gritted my teeth. "I'm going down to look for Dr. Diller," I said. "I have to save Poocher. Are you coming with me?"

Peter glanced around nervously. "Well, I'm not going to wait here all by myself."

"Okay. Come on," I said.

We went cautiously down the stairs. The door swung closed behind us. When we reached the bottom, I peered around in the weird red gloom, trying to figure out which way to go. Were there any doors down here?

Then I spotted something in the corner.

A cage. With something inside.

I crept closer—and saw a little brown puppy. He looked just like Poocher when I first got him.

I leaned down and peered into the cage. The puppy was sleeping.

"Oh, he's so sweet," I whispered. Without thinking, I opened the cage door and reached in.

And screamed.

Because when it glanced up at me, I saw that it wasn't a cute little dog at all.

It was a monster! A dog—with scales and a forked tongue!

The hideous beast hissed at me. I yanked my hand back.

I stared as its flat, furry head flared like a cobra's.

It reared up.

And bared snake fangs dripping with poison!

19

Before I could slam the door, something grabbed my arm.

I glanced down in horror.

The gruesome snake dog had wrapped its long, scaly tail around my wrist!

I shrieked and tugged as hard as I could. The snake dog held me tight. And it was about to strike!

"Peter! Help!" I hollered.

"Hold on! I'm coming!" he cried. I heard his sneakers slap the floor as he dashed toward me.

I tried to pull away from the cage, but the snake dog's tail held me tight. I yanked my arm hard.

The tail gripped me tighter.

The snake dog lashed out at my face.

I ducked. I felt the wind as its head whipped past, inches from my cheek.

Peter tore up and stomped hard on the base of the snake dog's tail. The snake dog hissed in pain. Its scaly grip loosened.

I yanked my arm free, slammed the cage door, and jumped back.

Then I collapsed on the floor, gasping.

"Are you okay, Maggie?" Peter demanded. "Hold on. I'll find a light switch."

He stumbled around in the darkness. A moment later I heard a click. A fluorescent light flickered on over our heads.

And we saw that the basement was filled with dog cages.

Monster-dog cages!

I grabbed Peter and held on tight. Both of us trembled as we gazed around the room.

There were monster dogs everywhere.

The weirdest, ugliest creatures I had ever seen!

One cage was covered with spiderwebs. A hideous spider dog waved its eight hairy legs through the bars. Each long spider leg ended in a clawlike paw. The dog's jaws were set sideways on its head. Like a spider's mandibles. They clacked open and shut.

The spider dog barked and shot a sticky strand of web at us.

Peter and I backed away in horror.

And bumped into another cage.

A flapping sound made us jump. We spun around and stared into the giant cage.

It was filled with bat dogs. Dogs with bat bodies. Their big, leathery wings flapped against the bars. They screeched and howled when they saw us.

We were trapped in a room full of monsters!

The cages rattled as the monster dogs barked and growled. And each monster dog was grosser than the last.

A lizard dog hissed.

A turtle dog snapped.

A vulture dog pecked.

"Wh-wh-what are they?" Peter stammered.

"They're gross!" I cried.

"But how . . . ?" Peter gripped my arm. "They're mutants! Like someone was trying to make new brands of dogs."

That's when the horrible truth hit me.

There was no way all these dogs could have gotten this way by accident. They had to be part of some terrible scientific experiment.

"Dr. Diller!" I exclaimed.

Dr. Diller must have done this!

"What? What about Dr. Diller?" Peter demanded.

I clutched his arm. I felt dizzy.

"Don't you get it?" I said hoarsely. "Poocher isn't sick. He's an experiment!"

Peter's eyes widened. "You mean—?"

"Yes," I whispered.

Dr. Diller was behind it all!

I couldn't believe it. We came here for her help.

Some help!

The monster dogs threw themselves against the

bars. Their cages rattled loudly. They squeaked and howled.

It sounded as if we had stepped into a zoo. And all the animals were going crazy!

"Let's get out of here!" Peter shrieked.

He dashed to a heavy steel door on the far wall and tried to open it.

It didn't budge.

The cages rattled even louder.

The monster dogs were trying to escape!

A black-and-white-spotted monkey dog reached its fingers through the cage. It picked at the lock.

"Peter! Look!" I gasped.

We stared at the monkey dog. He looked like a dalmatian crossed with a chimpanzee. His eyes glowed with intelligence. He screeched and wagged his long tail.

Then he reached through the bars with long, fingerlike paws. He snatched a paper clip from the floor.

Peter must have dropped it. Weird stuff is always falling out of his pockets.

With one smooth twist, the monkey dog used the paper clip to unlock the door of his cage!

"He's free!" I hollered to Peter.

The monkey dog screeched in triumph. Then he leapt on top of another cage. He flung open the door.

An alligator dog crawled out and snapped its jaws.

Peter tugged frantically at the steel door. I grabbed his arm and pointed back at the stairway.

"The way we came!" I screamed. "Run for it!"

Peter ducked and bolted for the stairs. I followed right behind him.

"Hurry! Hurry!" I shrieked.

More cage doors exploded open. More monster dogs burst free. They swarmed after us.

Peter and I screamed and tore up the stairs. The monster dogs scurried up behind us.

At the top of the stairs I grabbed the doorknob and shoved as hard as I could.

The door wouldn't move.

It was stuck!

We were doomed!

We were monster-dog food!

20

The monster dogs barked and screeched. They were about to attack. And we had nowhere to run.

"Push, Peter! Push!" I yelled furiously.

Peter and I threw ourselves against the door.

It flew open.

We tumbled into the dark hallway of the clinic. I tried to slam the door behind me.

A thick, scaly alligator tail whipped through before I could get the door all the way closed.

Peter and I pressed with all our weight against the door. But there were lots of monster dogs pushing on the other side. And they were stronger than we were.

Slowly, slowly, the door began to creak open.

And then I heard a voice behind me. A voice that chilled my blood.

"What on earth—?"

It was Dr. Diller!

She must have heard the racket from wherever she was working. She strode up beside Peter and me, carrying a squat black box in her hand. She didn't even glance at us. She just shoved the box against the alligator tail.

Zzzt! Blue sparks shot from two metal prongs at the end of the box. I heard a weird, bubbling howl from the stairs. The tail vanished back inside.

Dr. Diller slammed the door and slid the bolt into place.

The monster dogs howled and threw themselves against the locked door. But Dr. Diller ignored the noise. She turned and studied Peter and me as if we were insects in a jar.

"Good evening, Maggie," she said calmly. "How's Poocher?"

Peter and I gaped up at her.

We were safe from the monster dogs. But not from Dr. Diller. After all, she had turned Poocher into a monster.

And now that we knew her secret, what would she do to us?

I had to think fast.

"Dr. D-D-Diller!" I stammered. "Uh—you must be wondering what we're doing here. Well, our mom will explain everything to you. She's waiting outside in the car. We—um—we better get going before she gets worried."

Dr. Diller didn't fall for it. "I see you've met my pets," she murmured. "I'm afraid I can't let you leave now."

She shoved her hands into her lab coat pockets and gazed thoughtfully from me to Peter.

Uh-oh. Obviously, bluffing wasn't going to work.

"Pets?" I shouted. "They're monsters! That's what you do here, isn't it? You make people's pets into monsters!"

Dr. Diller stepped toward us. Her hands were still in her pockets.

"Oh, I wouldn't call them monsters. Though it is true they aren't very well behaved," she admitted. "They haven't been properly trained yet. Not like Poocher. He's a good dog, isn't he, Maggie?"

My anger flared up. "He's no dog. He's a monster too! I felt so terrible. I thought I made Poocher sick when I gave him the wrong food. But it was all your fault!" I shouted.

"You gave him something other than my special formula? I warned you about that," Dr. Diller scolded. She clicked her tongue. "Impure food can trigger certain . . . changes. My formula was supposed to keep Poocher's genetic alteration under control. That is, until I chose otherwise."

"What did you do to my Poocher?" I demanded.

"My dear," Dr. Diller said, raising her eyebrows, "you should be grateful. I gave him back to you—*improved.*"

"Improved?" I cried. "He's got huge claws and fangs and glowing red eyes!"

Dr. Diller nodded. "The perfect watchdog," she said proudly. "Let me explain. I am a scientist. My experiments combine the genes of different animals. In other words, I create brand-new creatures."

"You create monsters," I retorted.

Dr. Diller glared at me coldly. "Some people might say that," she responded. "Many thought my experiments were cruel. They said I was mad."

"No kidding," Peter muttered.

Dr. Diller frowned. "Great scientists are often thought to be mad," she said briskly. "But one day I'll show everyone. I will create a perfect race of super-animals."

Peter and I gulped.

"That's why I came to Shadyside," Dr. Diller continued. "I needed a place where no one knew me. A place where I could get my hands on all the animals I needed."

"Like Poocher," I groaned.

"Yes, like Poocher," Dr. Diller agreed. "Your improved Poocher is one of my greatest successes. So much smarter than normal dogs. Stronger too. And so loyal."

Tears welled up in my eyes. "Poocher was perfect before you turned him into a . . . a . . ." I choked on my words.

"A wonderful new species," Dr. Diller finished for me. "A dog—crossed with a lion, a shark, and a porcupine."

"No!" I wailed. "Oh, Poocher!"

Dr. Diller circled us slowly. Peter reached for my hand and clasped it. His hand trembled. Or maybe it was mine—I'm not sure.

"She's crazy, Maggie," he whispered. "Totally wacko! What is she going to do with us?"

I didn't even want to think about it. My heart raced as I scanned the hallway.

Our only hope was to make a run for it. Maybe we could reach the front door before she caught up with us.

"Okay," I whispered. "One. Two—"

I never got to three.

Dr. Diller leapt behind us. In a flash, she snapped something around our necks.

Dog collars!

We were Dr. Diller's prisoners!

She tugged hard on the leashes. Peter and I stumbled backward.

"This way, my pets," she commanded. She pulled us down the hall toward a red door.

"Wh-where are you taking us?" Peter stammered.

Dr. Diller pulled out a ring of keys. "My laboratory, of course," she answered.

I didn't like the sound of that. "Why?" I asked fearfully.

Dr. Diller unlocked the red door and turned to face us.

"Can't you guess?" she asked with a gentle smile. "I'm ready to move on to a new level in my experiments.

"And you two will be my first test subjects."

21

I felt the blood drain from my face.

"No!" I gasped.

"You can't!" Peter cried.

"Oh, but I can," Dr. Diller corrected us. She pushed the red door open. "Welcome to my laboratory."

She tugged on our leashes. Peter and I stumbled inside. We squinted in the glare of bright lights.

Soon my eyes adjusted. I gazed around the room.

Tons of shiny steel equipment cluttered the lab. Weird machines buzzed and whirred. Computer screens glowed.

A huge metal frame was bolted to the far wall. It looked like a giant jungle gym—with hundreds of test tubes attached.

Thick, gloppy fluid bubbled in each of the tubes.

Peter tugged my arm and pointed across the room. "Look!"

I stared. Dozens of steel cages lined the walls. A different animal paced back and forth inside each cage.

A tiger. A rat. A snake. And lots more.

Long tubes and wires flowed from each cage.

What was Dr. Diller doing to these poor animals?

"This is horrible!" I blurted out.

Dr. Diller frowned. "This is the future, Maggie," she said crisply. "Soon every family in America will own one of my special pets."

"You're crazy!" I shouted. "You're crazy and cruel and evil!"

"I am a scientist," she snapped. "Enough of this nonsense. It's time to begin the experiment."

"Wh-what do you mean?" I stammered.

Dr. Diller pointed to a large lab table in the middle of the room. Leather straps crisscrossed the table. Wires hung down from the ceiling. A giant steel claw loomed overhead.

"I've never experimented on a human before," Dr. Diller announced. Her voice was cold. Unemotional.

A shock of terror jolted up my spine.

"Wait! You don't want to do this!" I cried.

"Yes, I do," Dr. Diller retorted. "Tonight, with your help, I will make history."

Dr. Diller looped Peter's leash around a hook set high in the wall. Then she pulled me toward the lab table.

"No!" I shrieked. I tugged at the collar with all my strength.

It was no use. Dr. Diller jerked the leash until the collar tightened around my neck. I started to choke.

Dr. Diller shoved me onto the lab table. She fastened the leather straps around my arms and legs.

"Don't worry, Maggie," she whispered in my ear. "You are contributing to one of the greatest experiments of all time. You should be honored. And you will be rewarded."

I screamed.

I struggled against the straps.

No use.

I was going to become one of Dr. Diller's monster animals! What was she going to combine me with? The tiger? The rat?

Would I even survive?

She pressed a button and a small steel dome descended from the ceiling. She placed it on my head.

"You're the real monster, Dr. Diller!" I shrieked.

"We'll see about that, won't we?" she muttered.

Then she turned and reached for a bunch of long wires. One by one, she hooked them up to other long wires.

Wires from the animal cages.

I glanced at Peter. He yanked and tugged on his leash. But he couldn't escape.

"Stop it!" he wailed. "Leave my sister alone!"

Dr. Diller spun around. "Don't worry," she grated, aiming her finger at Peter. "You're next."

She turned back to me. "Now everything is ready."

My heart nearly stopped.

Dr. Diller raised her hand over my face. Her finger pushed a button on the steel dome.

Peter shouted, but I could barely hear him. Something was buzzing in my head.

I closed my eyes and screamed.

"Noooo!!!"

My cry echoed in the lab.

And the echo was answered.

With a bark.

It sounded like . . . Poocher!

I screamed again.

"Poocher! Help me!" I shrieked.

I heard growling and snarling.

I opened my eyes.

The red door of the lab burst open with a loud crash.

And Poocher leapt inside!

I couldn't believe my eyes.

Poocher was the biggest, meanest monster dog of them all!

He stood nearly eight feet high. His whole body bulged with massive muscles. His coat rippled with razor-sharp quills.

His gleaming claws made a *snick! snick!* sound against the floor. Like knives.

His massive jaws snapped at the air. His fangs were huge. His eyes burned red and bright.

Poocher fixed his glowing red eyes upon Dr. Diller. He roared.

"Get back!" Dr. Diller cried. "Heel, Poocher. Heel!"

But Poocher didn't heel. He paced toward the doctor, snarling.

Yes!

Poocher was on our side! He was protecting me!

He was going to save us!

"Get her, boy!" I cheered.

"No!" Dr. Diller stepped backward and bumped into a cage.

Poocher growled. And leapt!

Dr. Diller screamed in horror. The monster dog tackled her to the floor. She struggled beneath him.

Suddenly there was a hideous burst of screeching in the hall. A moment later, all the monster dogs burst into the lab. They must have escaped from the basement.

And they were very, very mad.

At Dr. Diller.

Dr. Diller screamed even louder. Her cold blue eyes bulged when she saw the monster dogs.

Then they attacked!

The bat dogs flew at her neck. The monkey dog pinned her to the floor. The spider dog crawled over her face.

And that was just the beginning.

Soon Dr. Diller was completely covered with monster dogs. They clawed and nipped and buzzed and scratched. I couldn't even see Dr. Diller anymore.

But I could still faintly hear her terrified screaming.

Poocher jumped away from the other monster dogs. He sniffed the air. Then he turned toward me. His red eyes glared at me.

"Poocher, it's me," I cried. "Maggie. Help me!"

He dashed across the lab and leapt up on the table.

He tore at the leather straps with his fangs.

I was free! I yanked the steel cap off my head.

"Yes! Poocher!" I hooted.

Jumping up, I threw my arms around his neck.

He might be a monster. But he was *my* monster.

His quills didn't bother me at all.

"Come on, Poocher, boy," I urged after a second. "We have to help Peter."

Poocher seemed to understand. He galloped across the lab to Peter. He lashed out with one tremendous claw and sliced through Peter's leash.

Peter was free!

I rushed to my little brother and hugged him tight.

"Good boy!" Peter cheered. He thumped Poocher on the back.

A loud scream made us all turn.

Dr. Diller crawled out from under a pile of monster dogs. Her lab coat was shredded. She pushed her hideous creations aside and stumbled out of the room.

The monster dogs went after her.

We watched Dr. Diller race down the hall to the open front door. She bolted into the darkness.

And the monster dogs followed her.

We heard their howls—and Dr. Diller's screams—fade into the night. Soon they were gone.

I wondered if we'd ever hear from them again.

Frankly, I didn't care. We were safe. We were free.

"Let's get out of here," I said to Peter.

I hopped onto Poocher's back. Peter jumped up behind me.

"Giddyap, Poocher!" I whooped.

Poocher barked. It sounded like a tiger's roar.

He charged down the hall and leapt through the front doorway.

Off we galloped, into the night. Through the dark streets of Shadyside. We laughed and cheered all the way home.

Of course, Poocher had to stop and howl at the moon a few times.

After all, he's still only a puppy.

22

"I wish I could go to the park with you and Poocher," Peter complained. "But I'm grounded. As usual."

It was a week later. Peter and I sat in the kitchen after school.

"Oh, well," I said. "Another time."

I was glad that Peter wasn't jealous of Poocher anymore. In fact, we had lots of fun together now. All three of us.

"Poocher really is a good dog," I mused. "Now that we understand him."

"Yeah," Peter agreed, reaching for the bag of cookies on the table. "It just took some getting used to. Having a dog and everything."

"Especially one as special as Poocher," I added.

The doggy door swung open. Poocher trotted inside. He wagged his tail and dashed to the pantry door. He grabbed his leash from the knob. Then he dropped it on my lap.

I laughed. "I guess it's time for our walk, huh?"

Poocher yipped.

"I guess he showed you who's boss," Peter joked.

"We'll be back in a little while. See you later," I called to my brother. Then I snapped the leash onto Poocher's collar. Together we strolled outside and headed down Fear Street.

Poocher trotted along happily. He sniffed the flowers. He chased the butterflies.

He was so cute!

We paraded past Billy Caldwell's house. Billy was just coming out of his yard. Bullhead ambled beside him.

They took one look at us and hurried across the street. Billy's face was pale under the freckles.

I smiled down at Poocher. "I'm so glad Billy and Bullhead have stopped bothering us. Aren't you, Poocher?"

Poocher yipped.

I knew what he meant. He didn't care about Billy and Bullhead. He just wanted to play.

And I knew what his favorite game was.

My teeth grew long and pointy.

My eyes glowed red.

"All right, Poocher," I said. "Let's play!"

Are you ready for another walk
down Fear Street?
Turn the page for a terrifying
sneak preview.

R.L. STINE'S
GHOSTS OF FEAR STREET® #25

HALLOWEEN BUGS ME!

Coming mid-September 1997

"Greg! Look!" Liv screamed. She stared across the room in horror.

I followed her gaze—and screamed too.

My cat was crawling inside the magic trick-or-treat bag.

"Princess, NO! Get out of there!" I dove for the bag.

Too late.

She was completely inside it.

I tried to grab the bag—but I couldn't.

It leaped around on the floor. It jerked wildly from side to side. Snarls and hisses filled the air.

"Wow!" Raina, my little sister, stared wide-eyed. "It sounds like Princess is fighting another cat in there!"

I really hoped she was wrong.

Finally, I pounced on the bag. I lay on top of it. It jerked and twitched for a second. Then it stopped.

My heart pounded as I sat up and let go.

Princess scrambled out.

Followed by another Princess.

And another Princess. And another. And another. And another.

"Oh, *noooo!*" I moaned.

The magic bag had done it again.

Only this time, it multiplied Princess!

I watched in horror as ten white cats filled my room.

One jumped on my desk and pawed at my glass baseball trophy.

It started to topple.

"Greg!" Liv screamed. "Get it!"

I leaped across the room—and caught the trophy before it fell. "Whew! That was close! But I got it." I said, holding it up.

"Not that!" she hollered. "The bag!"

I whirled around—and saw two cats crawl back into the bag. The bag jerked and hopped across the room. It was totally out of control!

The second I wrestled it to the ground, twenty more cats scrambled out!

"Oh, nooooo," I moaned. "Thirty cats!"

Now I had *thirty* cats in my small room.

Cats creeping on my desk, stretching on my bed, tiptoeing along on my bookshelves, padding across my drum set.

Every inch of carpet covered with cats. So many they couldn't walk without bumping into each other.

They swarmed around my ankles, meowing.

I tried to move away, but I couldn't. There was no place to go without stepping on a cat.

"Wow!" Raina's eyes opened wide in amazement. "You're in trouble now, Greg!"

"Get them!" I yelled.

Liv and I ran around the room, trying to gather up the cats. I scooped one up—and it gave a long, menacing hiss.

Whoa! Princess would never do that!

"Ow!" Liv screamed. I whirled around to look at her. Another cat sank its teeth into her ankle.

I picked up a third cat.

I cuddled it in my arms. "Nice kitty," I murmured. "Nice Princess."

It let out a long, throaty purr—then swiped its claws across my cheek.

"Owww!" I dropped the cat and ran my hand over my cheek.

Blood! There was blood trickling from my raw skin!

"Watch out, Greg! Behind you!" Liv yelled.

I whirled around—just in time to dodge a cat leaping from the dresser. It was aiming for my head, but it landed on my leg. Clung to it. Sank its sharp claws into my shin.

Another cat flew at me. It landed on my chest. I jerked my head back—as it tried to scratch my eyes out.

"These cats aren't like Princess." Raina whimpered. She shrank back as two hissing cats moved in on her. "These cats are mean. Me and my hamster are going back to my room." Cradling her hamster in her hands, she darted out.

Thirty terrifying cats tore at my bedspread. My curtains. My carpet. They batted my books off the shelves. They ripped my homework to shreds. They chewed through my pillow.

"There's something wrong with these cats!" I cried. "They're vicious! It's the bag's fault! They're *not* like Princess! The trick-or-treat bag changed them!"

Liv backed herself against a wall. "This isn't working," she shouted. "We can't pick up these cats!"

I shielded my face with my hands as another cat hurled itself at me.

"What else can we do?" I wailed. "We have to pick them up! We can't just leave them here! Do you have a better idea?"

Liv peeled a cat off her leg and gazed at me with narrowed eyes. "Yes, I do," she said. "I have an idea—but you're not going to like it."

"Try me," I begged. "I'll do *anything!*"

"Muffin? Use that crazy dog Muffin to get rid of the cats! No way!" I declared.

We were standing in the hall outside my room. Inside, thirty cats yowled and scratched at the door. Liv had grabbed the magic trick-or-treat bag while I cleared a path to the door.

"It's the *only* way," Liv insisted. "The way to get rid of cats is with dogs. The dogs will chase the cats out! If you have a better idea—let's hear it!"

I didn't have a better idea—so we sneaked out of my house and over to Mrs. O'Connor's yard.

Muffin was lying on the walkway. The second he caught sight of us he let out a growl. His lip curled back to bare his teeth.

"I don't like this," I muttered, staring at him. Muffin was little, but he was mean.

"We have no choice," Liv reminded me. "Do you remember the plan?"

I nodded. The plan. That was what had me worried.

Liv marched up to Muffin.

He trained his eyes on her. Watching her. Waiting to see what she was up to.

I tiptoed up behind him—and threw the trick-or-treat bag over him.

"Arf! Grff! Rowf!" Inside the bag, Muffin erupted in furious barks and snarls.

"Got him!" I cried. "Let's go!"

Liv helped me scoop the bag up.

I held it closed—but it wasn't easy. Muffin struggled like a maniac.

We started back to my house. Liv held up the bottom of the bag. I clutched the top. Muffin barked madly.

"Hurry! Run. Before Mrs. O'Connor hears him!" Liv grunted.

Mom and Dad were in the living room, near the front door—so we had to sneak in through the back.

"What's all that noise?" Mom called to us as we struggled up the steps with the bag.

"Just a new CD Liv's playing on her portable

stereo," I answered, gasping for breath. "Sorry. We'll lower the volume."

We reached my bedroom. I threw open the door.

We dropped the bag on the floor—and ten furious Muffins burst out of the bag.

Luckily for us, the dogs forgot all about us the moment they spotted the cats. The dogs eyed their prey in menacing silence.

The cats returned their gaze. Their fur bristled. They arched their backs.

I hope this works, I prayed. It's got to work. It's just got to!

The dogs curled back their lips.

They bared their fangs.

They opened their jaws—

And *quacked!*

About R.L. Stine

R.L. Stine is the best-selling author in America. He has written more than one hundred scary books for young people, all of them best-sellers.

His series include *Fear Street, Ghosts of Fear Street* and the *Fear Street Sagas.*

Bob grew up in Columbus, Ohio. Today he lives in New York City with his wife, Jane, his teenage son, Matt, and his dog, Nadine.

Pocket Books /"Monster Dog" Sweepstakes!

Is Your Pup Truly Terrifying?

Win a Photo Spot in Ghosts of Fear Street® #36

and

A "Pawtographed" Photo of R.L. Stine
and His Monster Dog, Nadine

1 Grand Prize

A photo of you and your creepy canine will be featured in R.L. Stine's Ghosts of Fear Street® #36 (on sale mid-August 1998). Plus, you'll win 25 copies of the book (approximate total retail value $100) and a "pawtographed" photo of R.L. Stine and his dog, Nadine.

25 Second Prizes

25 second place winners will receive a "pawtographed" photo of R.L. Stine and his dog, Nadine.

Child's Name________________ Birthdate___/___/__

Parent's Name____________________________

Address________________________________

City____________________ State______ Zip_____

Phone(_____) _________________________

A Minstrel® Book

1407 (1of2)

POCKET BOOKS/"GOFS Monster Dog" SWEEPSTAKES

Official Rules

1. No Purchase Necessary. Enter by mailing the completed Official Entry Form (no copies allowed) and a photograph of yourself and your "monster dog" or by mailing the photograph and a 3" x 5" card with your name and address to the Pocket Books/Monster Dog Sweepstakes, 13th Floor, 1230 Avenue of the Americas, NY, NY 10020. Entries must be received by 3/1/98. Not responsible for lost, late, stolen, illegible, mutilated, incomplete, postage due or misdirected entries or mail or for typographical errors in the entry form or rules. Enter as often as you wish, but one entry per envelope. Winners will be selected at random from all eligible entries received in a drawing to be held on or about 3/1/98. All entries become the property of Pocket Books, a division of Simon & Schuster, Inc.
2. Prizes: One Grand Prize: A picture of the winner and the winner's horrifying hound featured in R.L. Stine's Ghosts of Fear Street® #36: (on sale in mid-August 1998). Winner will also receive 25 copies of the book (approximate total retail value $100) and a "pawtographed" photo of R.L. Stine and his dog Nadine.
25 Second Prizes: 25 second place winners will receive a "pawtographed" photo of R.L. Stine and his dog Nadine.
3. The sweepstakes is open to residents of the U.S. and Canada, excluding the province of Quebec, not older than fourteen as of 3/1/98. Proof of age required to claim prize. Prizes will be awarded to a winner's parent or legal guardian. Void in Puerto Rico and wherever prohibited or restricted by law. Simon & Schuster, Inc., Parachute Publishing, L.L.C., and their respective officers, directors, shareholders, employees, suppliers, parents, subsidiaries, affiliates, agencies, sponsors, participating retailers, and persons connected with the use, marketing or conduct of this sweepstakes and their families living in the same household, are not eligible.
4. One prize per person or household. Prizes are not transferable and may not be substituted except by sponsor, in event of unavailability, in which case a prize of equal or greater value will be awarded. All prizes will be awarded. The odds of winning a prize depend upon the number of eligible entries received.
5. If a winner is a Canadian resident, then he/she must correctly answer a time-limited, skill-based question administered by mail.
6. All expenses on receipt and use of a prize including Federal, state and local taxes are the sole responsibility of the winners. Winners will be notified by mail. Winners may be required to execute and return an Affidavit of Eligibility and Release and all other legal documents which the sweepstakes sponsor may require (including a W-9 tax form) within 15 days of receipt of notification or an alternate winner will be selected.
7. By accepting a prize winners or winner's parents or legal guardians, as applicable, irrevocably grant Pocket Books, Parachute Publishing L.L.C., and Simon & Schuster, Inc. the worldwide right, for no additional consideration, to use their names, photographs, likenesses, and entries for any advertising, promotion, marketing and publicity or any other purpose without further compensation to or permission from the entrants, except where prohibited by law.
8. Winners agree that Simon & Schuster Inc., and Parachute Publishing, L.L.C., and their respective officers, directors, shareholders, employees, suppliers, parents, subsidiaries, affiliates, agencies, sponsors, participating retailers, and persons connected with the use, marketing or conduct of this sweepstakes, shall have no responsibility or liability for injuries, losses, or damages of any kind in connection with the collection, acceptance or use of the prizes awarded herein.
9. By participating in this sweepstakes, entrants agree to be bound by these rules and the decisions of the judges and sweepstakes sponsors, which are final in all matters relating to the sweepstakes.
10. For a list of prize winners, (available after 3/15/98) send a stamped, self-addressed envelope to Prize Winners, Pocket Books/Monster Dog Sweepstakes, 13th Floor, 1230 Avenue of the Americas, NY, NY 10020.

1407 (2of2)